D0166545

A Broken Race

A Broken Race

JEAN DAVIS

All rights reserved. No part of this book may be reproduced or transmitted in any forms or by any means without prior written consent from the author excepting brief quotes used in reviews.

These stories are works of fiction. Names, characters, places, and incidents are the product of the author's imagination or are used fictitiously Any resemblance to actual persons, living or dead, events, or locals is entirely coincidental

Copyright © 2015 Jean Davis

First Edition October 2015 Caffeinated Press
Second Edition March 2018

ISBN: 978-1985732407

A NOTE FROM THE AUTHOR

Joshua's story would still be languishing on my hard drive if it weren't for my critique partners— Bedrich Pasek VII, Susan A. Royal, Kathryn Sparrow, and Joy Basham—who helped me put what was in my head onto the page. Also, a big thank you to my Caffeinated Press editing team, who saved the world from eight pages of characters eating crackers. Don't ask, just be grateful.

This new edition includes additional content that readers asked for. I love to hear from readers. I also like reviews. If you are so inclined, please consider leaving one.

I hope you enjoy this expanded edition.

PROLOGUE

Nickolas yelped as his favorite aide fell to the floor. Blood gushed from his nose.

"Mr. Forrest, are you okay?"

The middle-aged man grasped his throat with both hands, his face turning red with white blotches. "Get help."

Nickolas ran from his room and down the hall. All around him, people in white uniforms like Mr. Forrest were sprawled across the floor. Most of them had been there for weeks. Most of them were dead.

The sickness worked faster in some than others. He dodged a pair of hands that tried to catch the leg of his pants as he went by. Flies buzzed around his face. His eyes watered and his stomach clenched. The doorway used to be his favorite place. There, he could watch the people who would come to visit his friends. Now it gave him nightmares.

Mr. Forrest had assured Nickolas that he wasn't going to get sick like the others, but now there wasn't anyone else left to take care of him and that brought on a panic that shook his whole body. He tried to breathe like the therapist taught him to, but it was hard. All he wanted to do was curl up in a dark corner and close his eyes. But Mr. Forrest needed help.

Wrapping his arms across his chest, his habitual rhythmic nod took up a silent beat. He forced himself to keep walking.

Amanda sat at the desk by the courtyard where Mr. Sam, who kept them safe inside the home, used to sit. He'd left days ago, and he'd taken the keys with him.

Mr. Forrest wanted to go home to his wife and two boys. He hadn't been happy about getting locked in. None of them were. But Mr. Sam said it was for their own good. The television showed riots in the streets, buildings burning, bodies outside in piles. Inside might be safer, but Nickolas longed for the fresh air and sunshine of the courtyard.

He frowned at the blue coat she wore over her pink shirt. "You shouldn't wear Mr. Sam's coat. He'll be mad."

"He's dead. Like everyone else." She pulled her knees up to her chest and wrapped her arms around them. Her big blue eyes looked up at him through blonde bangs that hung almost to the tip of her nose.

"We don't know that. He's not here."

"Jackson said so." Tears welled in her eyes.

"Where is he? Mr. Forrest needs help."

She pointed to the day room where they often played games together. "He's talking to a strange man that came in."

"How? The doors are all locked."

She whispered, "He had the keys."

There was only one body in the hallway to the day room. Most of the staff had gone to the doors. A few had made it out before Mr. Sam had locked them inside. Some of Nickolas's friends had too, their families coming for them soon after the first people started to get sick.

No one had come for him. Mr. Forrest said it was probably because his family was scared or sick, but Nickolas knew it was because they didn't like him. That's why they paid for him to live here instead of at home with them. If he was here, they didn't have to look at him or make him stay in his room when people were over.

Nickolas smiled, his father couldn't yell at him here. This home was better than theirs.

The virus had moved through the home in days, making almost everyone sick, friends and staff. Only the three of them didn't get the fever that was the first sign of getting sick.

Nickolas found Jackson talking to a man with very dark skin and snow white hair. It must have been important because Jackson had his earphones around his neck. Not just one ear open to hear, with the earphones twisted in his hair like he usually did, but completely off.

Music kept him calm. Everyone wanted Jackson, who was taller and wider than even Mr. Sam, to stay calm. The last time he'd gotten angry, it had taken five of the staff to hold him down before they could give him medicine to make him happy again.

Nickolas shivered. There weren't five people

here anymore and none of them knew how to do the medicines except Mr. Forrest. And now he was sick.

"Nickolas." Jackson waved him over.

The old man smiled at him. "Hello, I'm Father Frederick. Mr. Sam sent me to get all of you."

Shuffling footsteps signaled Amanda creeping up on them. "He's not dead?" she asked hopefully.

"I came from a hospital. Where sick people go," said Father Frederick. "He was there."

Nickolas tried not to imagine nice Mr. Sam all bloody and blackened on the floor like all the others. He pictured clean white sheets and smiling nurses. "He's safe then, in the hospital?"

Father Frederick took a long time to answer, looking at all of them slowly before taking a deep breath and letting it out. "How much have you seen of what is going on outside?"

"We watched the news," said Jackson proudly.

"Yes, then you've seen. Atlanta is in a state of emergency, or it was. Not enough people are alive to care much about that anymore." A sad smile took over his face.

Father Frederick pulled a small black book from his pants pocket, clutching it with both hands. "There was a broadcast on the radio two nights ago. A call to bring all healthy survivors to a secure building outside the city. There are doctors there, and scientists, people to help keep you safe."

"Police?" asked Amanda.

"The army, I think, some of them anyway. Are there any more of you here?"

Jackson shook his head, shuffling the earphones around his neck.

"I'm sorry." As hard as the man was holding his book, Nickolas expected to see his fingers shove right through it. "Why don't the three of you go pack your things, and we'll get out of here. Would you like that?"

They all nodded. Amanda ran off in the direction of the women's wing while Nickolas and Jackson went the opposite way with Father Frederick trailing behind.

Mr. Forrest lay on the floor just like he'd been when Nickolas had left him, but he wasn't talking anymore. He wasn't moving either.

He'd been one of the fast ones, and that made Nickolas a little happy. He didn't know if he could stand Mr. Forrest reaching for him, trying to talk with his throat all swollen, so all he could do was make grunting and groaning noises.

Nickolas packed quickly and threw his clothes in the suitcase his mother had sent with him six years before. He gave Mr. Forrest one last glance before running all the way back to the day room to find the others. Jackson and Amanda were already waiting. Father Frederick led them out a back door, one they would have been yelled at for even trying to use if Mr. Sam had been there. But he wasn't.

The air smelled like smoke, but the sun warmed his shoulders. He smiled up at the blue sky, imagining the sounds of his friends playing the courtyard all around him. But they were gone too.

The only sounds were of their shoes on the sidewalk and Jackson humming softly to himself, his earphones still around his neck.

Father Frederick brought them to the parking lot where he opened the back door of a big white van. Four other people sat inside, young like the three of them. One of them wore a hospital robe, the others had real clothes. They all looked tired and worried.

"Hop in," Father Frederick said. "We've got a little over an hour drive ahead of us. Not too long and we'll be there."

Nickolas sat in the long back seat with Amanda on one side and Jackson on the other. They left the parking lot of the building where he'd lived the happiest years of his life and went out onto the road where he'd watched traffic speed by from the dayroom. There were no other cars moving on the road today, only a few empty ones off on the sides here and there.

"You're lucky to be on the outskirts of the city," said Father Frederick, looking back at them in the mirror as he drove. "It's much worse in the more populated areas. Some of those that have survived are helping others, taking them in, forming small communities to keep things running. Others aren't so kind, trying to take everything for themselves. We'll be lucky to have trained forces looking after us."

"Why doesn't everyone go where we are going?" asked one of the girls in the first row of seats.

"Because the doctors have asked for people like you. All of you. You're special, born the way you are.

The people we're going to see, they want to understand why most of you don't get the virus. They'll take good care of you, don't worry."

"You're staying with us, aren't you?" asked Amanda.

"If there's room for me. We'll see."

He drove the rest of the way in silence. The seven of them stared out the windows. Cars sat alongside the highway. Nickolas was pretty sure there were bodies in some them, but none of them were moving. An army truck passed them once, heading back toward the city. Two rows of soldiers sat in the back. One of them waved. He waved back.

The trees and grass alongside the road grew just like every other day, a little brown in the summer heat, but still pretty. Birds and butterflies flew around the bushes and flowers. Other than the music coming from Jackson's earphones, the ride was quiet and peaceful.

They passed through two smaller towns before more large buildings rose up in the distance. Two army trucks were parked across the road. Father Frederick slowed the van and then stopped in front of the soldiers.

He turned around. "I'll be right back. Everyone stay inside."

They watched as he spoke with two of the soldiers, pointing to the van now and then. One of the men in camouflage came over and poked his head inside. When he saw them, he smiled.

"Hello. We're glad you're here."

They all said hello, one of the boys in the front seat yelled but the rest mumbled or whispered.

Father Frederick came back inside a moment later. "We're almost there."

One of the trucks backed out of the way so they could continue down the highway. They turned off at the next exit, which brought them by farms with giant green fields. The farms gave way to small houses in rows alongside the road, much like the one Nickolas had grown up in, and a couple minutes later, a strip mall with colorful signs in the windows and a gas station. A soldier stood guarding the pumps. Turning there down a side street, they pulled to a stop in a giant parking lot in front of a big grey building. Rows of narrow dark windows lined the front. The parking lot held more army trucks and cars. Up in the front row, closest to the building was a row of shiny, fancy cars. Nickolas would have liked to look at his reflection in them, but four soldiers ran out to the van and told them to hurry.

They all grabbed their belongings and were rushed toward the door. Nickolas turned to see Father Frederick waving at them.

Jackson noticed too. He slowed and turned to female soldier beside them. "Why isn't he coming with us?"

"We're saving the space for people like you. There are more people he can help elsewhere."

Jackson watched Father Frederick get back in the van before he let the soldier continue their march across the lot.

Sad to see the nice man go but excited to see what awaited them inside, Nickolas hurried toward the door with the others. "Why are we walking so fast?" he asked her.

"Sorry, there are some people who are angry that you aren't sick like everyone else. They have guns." She glanced at the wooded area along the edge of the parking lot. "No one can hurt you once you're inside."

They piled up by the large metal door. More soldiers stood there, but they were smiling so he wasn't scared of them. One by one they filed inside. A man with a white shirt and blue tie sat at a desk just inside the door.

As each of them walked by, he wrote in a big book. When it was his turn, Nickolas paused in front of the man to give his name and birthday.

"Welcome, Nickolas Sutton." The man neatly wrote his name on a line of the back of the first page just below Jackson and Amanda. "May I see your hand, please?"

With a black marker, he wrote seventy-six on the back of Nickolas's left hand.

"What's this?"

"With so many of you here all at once, we're using numbers in order to keep our research organized until we can learn your names."

The line moved forward, bringing Nickolas into a grey stone hallway that ended in a brightly lit room with glass doors. Inside, two people covered in white suits from head to toe were talking to Amanda. The three of them moved away, walking into a mist. Minutes later, the door opened and Jackson went inside.

Nickolas's heart pounded, and he wasn't so sure about being excited anymore. He missed Mr. Forrest and his room at the home where he knew where everything was. His muscles began to twitch.

He noticed the nice soldier lady was still beside him. She patted his shoulder. "You're safe here. With all the smart people we have inside this building, we'll get this thing figured out, and you'll be able to go back out there as soon as it's safe. Don't worry, we'll take good care of you."

Feeling the twitching subside, Nickolas nodded. He stepped into the bright room and let the white-suited people lead him into the mist.

CHAPTER ONE

Jack peered into the darkness beyond the stone-and-wood wall, searching for any sign of Wildmen. The shuffle of boots on gravel drew his attention to the yard inside the fortress. A Simple looked up—moonlight reflecting in his wide, dull eyes—and said, "Sir, the perimeter is secure."

"Good work, One-fifty-two. Check it again." Jack waved the dependable young man off. He'd been under Jack's command for ten years, since turning eight, old enough to be responsible with orders.

"Yes, sir." With the same undaunted smile and nod with which he acknowledged every command, One-fifty-two ambled back to the gate door where a William would be waiting with keys to send him back out.

A flicker in the distance caught Jack's eye. Faint, then flaring, solidifying into a bright orb, the light barreled through the air with frightening speed. More pinpoints came to life in the night.

"We're under attack!" he yelled.

A burning arrow thwacked into the wall. Seconds later, four more joined it, dotting the upper wooden section of the wall with flickering flames. Calls of alarm sounded from his fellow Jacks stationed on the other walls.

Arrows arced overhead, gliding into the yard and finding purchase in the thatched roof of the Simples' bunkhouse.

"Get some Simples on that fire!" Jack said.

Simple men spewed from the burning building, tumbling out windows and stampeding through the doors on either end. One fell to the ground and clutched his knees, rocking, and wailing. Others just ran, terror driving them into running laps around the yard.

A portly William strode out of the dorm and shouted orders at the Simples.

Another arrow sailed overhead. Jack left the chaos inside the fortress to the William and drew his rifle.

Damned Wildmen must have timed the Simples' patrol runs. He'd have to talk to a William about that.

He peered through the scope and spotted the gray outlines of the ragged men and their bows. Jack fired. Precious bullets flew into the bushes. The deafening thunder of the rifle masked any screams of the wounded or dying. Just as well, he'd had never been fond of killing.

The rifles of the other three Jacks joined his in quelling the attack. The fires of the flaming arrows guttered out on the treated wood. Smoke from the dorms snaked up his nostrils. Jack let up on the trigger and coughed. He ejected the spent clip, pulled a new one from the belt slung across his chest, and rammed it home.

A William's high-pitched voice bellowed up with the smoke. "Protect the women!"

Jack did a quick count. Four Jacks on the walls. That left six more off duty who, having heard the alarm, would be circling the vault where the women lived. The women should be safe, but he couldn't afford to be cocky about it. The women were more precious than the ever-dwindling stock of ammunition. Jack wiped away smoke-induced tears and peered through his scope.

A face loomed in front of him. A gaunt man with skin like leather leapt over the wall.

"They're on the walls," he called out.

Damn Wildmen, drawing attention to those in the distance, likely using their own Simples as disposable targets while the others crept closer with their ladders. He chided himself for falling prey to their tricks. Jack squeezed the trigger.

Bullets sank into each of the man's feet, ripping through his worn leather boots. He dropped onto the wooden walk.

Jack peered over the wall and finding the ladder, shoved it away. Screams and two heavy thuds followed seconds after.

"No!" cried the wounded Wildman. He pawed at the wall as if he could catch hold of the already fallen men.

"Stick around, old man, I'm sure a William would like to ask you a few questions." He spotted one of the fattest Williams attempting to corral three shrieking Simples who were running back and forth through the smoke. "Sir, I have a live one."

William-fourteen spared a glance at Jack and nodded. "Good work, Jack-three. Keep him subdued and hold your post. I'll speak with your captive when I'm done here."

Gunfire from the other three Jacks again filled the air. The rain of arrows ceased.

The Wildman shook his head, tears running down his face. "Please, we just want a woman or two. You have so many."

There weren't many, barely enough to produce a steady population in fact, and far too many of them Simples. "Your kind is full of the disease and filth that got us into this mess to begin with," Jack said.

The Wildman gritted his teeth, jagged things half hidden beneath an unruly beard. "You're blind, fortress-dweller. Brainwashed by your precious Williams and reveling in your power over those less fortunate."

"Without the Williams, we'd all be eating dirt and staring into the sun with stupid grins on our faces. You should be grateful for the progress they've made toward stabilizing our freefall into extinction, not harassing us with pathetic attempts to bring more Simples into the world."

"Look again." The Wildman squinted at him. "Are you a Jack or an Isaiah?"

The only Isaiah whom Jack had ever known had died three years ago. The Williams claimed he had been fifty-three. To live so long! Jack couldn't fathom the thought. He'd only glimpsed the Isaiah twice. With his withered dark skin and close-cropped white curls, he stood out from the others in the fortress. He spent most of his life sequestered away, working to find a cure to humanity's demise.

"A Jack."

"Fitting," the wounded man hissed. "I could be a Jack, you know. We're no different."

Jack snorted and checked the outlying area through his scope. Seeing nothing, he turned back to his captive. Sunken eyes, lips cracked and bleeding, the man glared up at him. Bruises and open sores showed through his thin, tattered clothes.

"You're nothing." Jack kicked him in the ribs.

The Wildman curled into a ball and moaned.

Seconds stretched to minutes as the ringing from the gunfire dissipated. Jack caught the shuffling of the Simples' feet as they worked to put out the fires. Given the comfort of the orderly task of carrying the buckets, their wailing had subsided. Jack wondered where One-fifty-two was and if he was all right.

Boots on the metal grate of the stairway below alerted Jack of his replacement's approach. The wide neck and heavy-jawed face of Jack-six popped up through the hatch in the walkway. "I hear you've got a live one."

The grin on his face worked its way up to his forehead, making his bare scalp crinkle around the edges. He poked at the Wildman with his boot.

The Jacks might have been brothers. Even

though their ages varied, they were similar in appearance. He often wondered if they all came from the same mother or if perhaps their father had been very successful in his breeding efforts.

Five more days and he'd be eligible for mating privileges. It'd been almost two months since his last night with a woman. One full week of a soft bed, plentiful meals, and all the sex he could manage. He felt a familiar stirring in his pants and grinned.

Jack set the rifle against the wall and unclipped his ammo belt. "They're all yours." He held out the belt to Jack-six. Once his hands were free, he hefted the wounded man onto his broad shoulders. "I doubt they'll try anything again tonight, but I'll take this one to a William and then we'll know for sure."

Jack-six nodded and picked up the rifle.

Jack-three made his way down the stairs and across the yard. The smoke had thinned but the stink still filled the air along with the lingering smell of gunpowder. Neither covered the rancid stench of the unwashed man on his back. He located a William in a crowd of Simples.

"Get back to your beds." William-fourteen shooed them away and peered at the Wildman with disdain. "Bring him to the jail. Remember to lock the cell."

Jack scowled. "I'm not a Simple, William."

"He treats you like you are. You don't need him," the Wildman said.

Jack clamped down on the scrawny man's legs and shoulder, driving his fingers into what little muscle the Wildman had. "Shut up."

The man squealed and squirmed in his grasp.

William's lips drew thin and his brows lowered though his voice remained calm and even. "Of course you aren't a Simple, Jack. I didn't mean to imply that you were. Once the prisoner is secure, you may turn in for the night. I'll see about moving up your reward week."

Muriel. Jack could feel the silken blonde locks in his hands, her smooth skin against his. "I want the same one. If moving me up the schedule means I won't get her, I'll wait."

William pulled a key from the ring he wore around his wrist and handed it to Jack. "Come see me when you're done with him and we'll discuss it."

As he walked, Jack's head swam with the clean scent of Muriel, the way she felt in his hands, the soft moans she made when he shared her bed.

The voice of the Wildman cut into his memories. "Slow down. You don't have to bring me to the jail, you know. You don't have to listen to that sack of hot air. We could make a deal, you and me. What do you say?"

He squeezed the man tighter.

The Wildman whimpered.

Jack worked his way through the moonlit streets deep within the fortress walls. Two more intersections and he stood in front of the jail. Its familiar rough walls were formed of row upon row of concrete chunks. He'd laid several of the rows himself back when he was in his early teens. His stomach rumbled with the distant memory of the extra rations his work had earned him.

"Use your brain, Jack. We both want the same thing. A woman. Or two. Maybe even three. You could handle three, couldn't you? You could, big strapping man like you. You could join us outside this place. I'd even let you have a go at them anytime you wanted. None of this weeks between sex crap the William's hold over your heads."

"Worry about your own head." As much as the thought of three women in his bed intrigued him, he couldn't allow the man to escape. Not after he'd seen the plantings and livestock. Even in the dark and thrown over his back, with pain likely clouding his vision, the man would have caught a glimpse of the lush gardens that fed the occupants of the fortress. Once the Wildmen had confirmation of what lay behind the walls, they'd try even harder to find a way in.

Jack unlocked the door and flipped on the light. Rats and roaches skittered for cover. He slid the Wildman off his back and dragged him into the nearest open cell.

The man gasped as Jack laid him on the floor. "You got a doctor? My feet hurt real bad."

"You won't live long enough to need one. William will see you shortly." Jack clicked the lock into place and left the doomed man behind.

He called out, "My name is Phillip."

"Your name means nothing to me." He flipped the light switch off.

Good thing they didn't allow Simples in the jail. Men like this one would talk their ears off and fill their little brains with ideas they wouldn't know what to do with. If only the fortress were filled with able-minded men. Jack sighed, wondering what the world was like before it went to shit and Simples outnumbered the rest by twenty to one.

Jack locked the door behind him and hurried back to William-fourteen.

The Simple posted at the William's door waved, his gaping teeth forming a jack-o-lantern smile. "Hello, Jack."

"Hello, Three-twenty. William in?"

Three-twenty nodded. Jack went inside the cube of a house. The tin walls were rippled like the waves on the pond in the back corner of the fortress. Chipped sky-blue paint gave way to a rusty orange and a few large faded black letters. A metal desk with one corner propped on a stack of bricks, sat in the middle of the room. William sat behind it, his body covering any hint of what the chair itself might look like. He was bent over a book, each page a series of squares with names and numbers written in them. William tapped a pen against his chin and ignored Jack.

He set the key on the desk and waited for William to finish playing his I-am-more-important-than-you-are game. Jack gazed around the house, wishing he had one of his own. But he'd not had the fortune to be born with the mind of a William. Though he did well enough with the Simples in his charge, his talents did not lie in organization or motivation.

With the way the women were producing children, they'd be surrounded by Simples by the time he hit thirty or died, whichever came first. They needed a few generations of nothing but Isaiah's. They needed problem-solvers, thinkers, men who understood the precious journals and notes left by the Isaiah's who'd come before. That's what William claimed he was aiming for with the breeding records—working to undo the fact that the breeding pool had been reduced to mostly Simples. They were the ones who had been mostly immune to the virus long ago.

He shuddered, thinking of how much of their genes were a part of his. Though he'd been fortunate, how many of his own offspring would be born like them?

William finally looked up. He leaned back, set the pen on the desk and clasped his hands over his belly. "We're pleased with the result of your last breeding. As such, I would like to try you with the next breeder up the quality line. She has excellent genetics according to Isaiah's notes."

Relief rushed through him. He hadn't fathered a Simple. "I want the same one as last time." Muriel.

Women were worthy of their own names but the Williams wouldn't hear of it. They were all numbers, even the men, and that's the way Williams liked it. Easier to track, orderly, they said.

"You will do your duty and take the woman I

offer to you. She's ready right now."

Jack flexed his fingers, keeping them from forming fists. No doubt William would make note of any signs of open aggression in his file. Too many of those, he'd been warned, would result in his being pulled from breeding privileges. As much as the fortress didn't need more Simples, it also didn't need men who couldn't follow rules. Rule breakers were executed. He'd seen his share of unruly Simples put down over the years along with one old Jack who'd been fed up with the Williams' way of doing things. He had silently agreed with him, but Jack had no wish for a bullet to the head.

He took a deep breath and said, "If you were happy with the results from last time, why take a chance? Why not just keep me with the one I had before?"

William scowled, his chin dimpling with the downturn of his full lips. "Breeder sixty-three is not yet available for rotation. She won't be for another six months."

Jack's heart leapt. Muriel was still nursing and caring for their child. He could to meet his child, see it with his own eyes. He would know which one it was when it was old enough to leave the vault. He wouldn't have to guess like everyone else.

"I want her."

"You don't seem to understand."

"I do, you—"

He held up a hand. "Now, now, you know I don't mean it that way. It's just that, it's your job, as a viable breeder, to do what you can to make our people successful for future generations. You can't let your emotions get involved."

Jack did know. His shoulders slumped.

"Don't be discouraged." William smiled. "Who knows, maybe you'll earn another reward by the time breeder sixty-three becomes available."

He didn't fool himself into believing a word the William's straight, white teeth and slippery tongue tried to sell him. He'd exposed his attachment to Muriel. William would note it in his file. Jack would never end up with her again. Men with emotional attachments were unpredictable, and that led to chaos according to what the William's preached.

"Yes, William."

"Thank you for understanding." William's smile became a touch more genuine. He picked up his pen and filled in an empty square on his page: Jack-three with Breeder Seventy-one, September 24, 2139. "You know the way. I'll have William-two meet you at the vault to let you in. Enjoy your week off."

Jack stopped off at the barracks he shared with the other nine of his designation. He packed his things into the basket he kept under his bed. When no one was looking, he pulled up his mattress and pulled out two lengths of the thin metal rod he'd found on a salvage run in the wildlands six months ago. He put them in his boot.

He'd also found a book on picking locks and had spent a good amount of time he should have been herding the Simples on the run with him, reading it. There were a lot of locks in the fortress, locks only Williams had keys to, and that had never set right with him or the other Jacks. Too many secrets. There were also too many Williams, which limited his practice with the rods. However, with a week, and only one William at the vault door, he'd have plenty of time to find his way to Muriel and their child.

Beside where he'd hidden the rods, lay a wrapped package that fit neatly into his palm. Muriel liked the color blue. He'd found the perfect stone on one of his runs last month. He unwrapped the tattered white cloth to behold his handiwork. Silver wire encaged a stone as big as the end of his thumb. It hung from a black cord. He couldn't wait to tie it around her neck, to see it resting on her smooth white skin.

He wrapped the necklace back in the cloth and shoved it deep into his pocket. No words on paper, or know-it-all fat men, were going to keep him away from what was rightfully his.

With his shaving kit, a change of clothes, and a smile, Jack set off toward the vault.

CHAPTER TWO

One-fifty-two looked up at the charred hole above his bunk. The Wildmen had filled the bunkhouse with smoke. Though the gray haze was gone now, he coughed as he moved his belongings to a vacant lower bunk across the row. No rain would fall on him tonight. But bugs could come through the hole. Bats would fly in and land on him. He shuddered. Or rats. They would leave droppings in his bed and in his clothes. He sat on the edge of the mattress, rocking back and forth as he tried to make his thoughts quiet so he could sleep.

The puffy hand of a William landed on his shoulder. "Lie down, Simple."

One-fifty-two stilled under William's hand. Getting slapped wouldn't help him sleep any more than thoughts of rats and bats. He bowed his head and slid under his blanket to escape the William. After the man waddled down the row of bunks, One-fifty-two pulled his treasure from within the change of clothes stacked under his bed. He clutched the stuffed dog he'd found on his last scavenging run. The dog stank like smoke. He held it lower, pressing its comforting softness against his stomach. With his eyes squeezed shut, he lay there. Nothing happened. Sleep was hard like this when he was outside the fortress walls, but it was supposed to come easy when he was in his safe bed.

One-fifty-two listened to the breathing of his friends. Some of the very young boys were fresh from the vault. They whimpered beneath their blankets. He remembered the first time the Wildmen had attacked when he was little like them and didn't blame them for crying.

In the distance, he heard the baying of the guard dogs. The smoke and noise probably made them scared too.

He glanced around, spotting the William at the other end of the long, narrow building. The fat man grumbled as he walked; occasionally his voice rose enough that One-fifty-two could make out that he was yelling at one of the other Simples to stop crying and go to sleep.

The longer One-fifty-two lay there, the more he decided that he had to go to the outhouse. The second William who took the Simples outside during the night wasn't there. Maybe he had been hurt by a Wildman. That thought made him smile just a little.

One-fifty-two really had to go outside. He'd watched the Williams open the door enough times that he knew which locks had to be turned and which ones had to be slid.

He tucked the stuffed dog back under his clothes and grabbed his shoes. Under the safety of his blanket, he slipped them on.

His friends lay sleeping in their beds as he tip-toed past. One-fifty-two held his breath and worked his way toward the door.

He needed to breathe, but he wasn't outside yet. His lungs hurt. He gasped for a breath. Clenching his teeth together, he whipped his head around. William was far away with his back turned, bent over someone's bunk. One-fifty-two almost sighed with relief, but then caught himself. Outside. He could do that outside.

Slide the first lock. Turn the second lock. Reach way up high and flip the third lock upward. The fourth lock had to be pressed down real slow to keep quiet. He leaned on the door handle and pushed down. Click.

Cool night air hit One-fifty-two's face as he ducked out the door. He closed it softly behind him and ran. The moon was bright enough to light his way, but the deep shadows from the buildings hid him from the four Jacks on the walls. Always four Jacks up high. Walking, pacing, rubbing their hands together and checking their rifles.

One-fifty-two paused in the shadow of the outhouse and looked up at the wall. He didn't spot any Jacks, and if he couldn't see them, they couldn't see him. He slipped into the stinky box and relieved himself. When he was done, he quietly shut the door.

The dogs were still barking. The Williams assigned him to work with the dogs sometimes. They were soft and warm and not smoky smelling like his stuffed dog.

He wasn't tired yet. Maybe he could make the dogs feel better. One-fifty two went from shadow to shadow, not running, but walking real fast. If one of the Jacks saw him, they'd report him to a William. Then he'd be punished.

One-fifty-two was sick of Williams yelling at him and smacking him upside the head, of them always telling him what to do. Didn't he deserve to sleep good and be happy for a few minutes for all his hard work? Running patrols outside the walls for the Jacks was dangerous and it kept him up late, sometimes all night if the Williams ordered it. One-fifty-two scowled as he thought of the Williams posted at the patrol door, safe inside the fortress walls while he and his friends walked the pebbled paths looking for Wildmen and watching for bears.

He just wanted to pet the dogs for a little while. That wouldn't hurt anyone. One-fifty-two glanced back in the direction of the bunkhouse. One of the dogs howled. He set off toward the kennel again.

He passed the gardens where he worked with his friends three afternoons a week. There were tasty things in the garden. His stomach rumbled. Maybe just a quick snack and then he'd make his way to the kennel, but Williams didn't allow snacks—not for Simples. He sucked on his lips and hid beside the rain barrels next to the tool shed. What wouldn't the Williams miss in the garden? Beans? Williams couldn't have counted every single one. But the last one he'd snuck was seedy. The flat crispy peas were done. Corn tasted better cooked. Carrots! One-fifty-two grinned and slipped out from between the rain barrels.

The fence around the garden came to his shoulders. He ducked behind it. Vines, many of them brown now, covered the loose slats of wood. He nearly tripped over a wayward pumpkin.

"Stupid pumpkin." One-fifty-two shook his finger at the fruit like the Williams often did to him.

His stomach rumbled again. Carrots. Orange, crunchy, sweet. Saliva pooled in his mouth. He'd love to eat a handful, but that would be noticed. Maybe just two carrots then.

One-fifty-two leaned over, searching for the low, fluffy carrot greens. There! He bounded off toward the long frilly row. Kneeling down in the soft soil, he grabbed low on two of the carrot stalks and yanked. He could smell their earthy sweetness already.

Footsteps. Boots.

One-fifty-two dropped to his stomach in the dirt and wished himself small. He wasn't sure if that worked, but it made him feel better.

Boots on gravel. Closer. Right outside the garden fence.

One-fifty-two squeezed the carrots in his fists and shut his eyes.

Gravel crunched.

One-fifty-two peeked. One eye. Just a slit.

The moonlight shone off a bald head. Too thin for a William. Muscular. A shaved head. A Jack.

He cringed. If a Jack caught him out at night, he'd be beaten for sure.

CHAPTER THREE

The Jack whistled a familiar tune. One-fifty-two cracked open his other eye, peering into the shadows. The wide-shouldered shape of the man and sound of the footsteps were familiar too.

Jack-three looked down the road as he walked by. And he was smiling. He hardly ever smiled.

As he passed, One-fifty-two got to his knees. He and Jack-three were on the same shift. They should both be sleeping. One-fifty-two stood up, slow and careful. Quiet.

Jack-three kept going, farther and farther down the road. He might not be safe out here all alone. There could be Wildmen still hiding somewhere, just waiting for everyone to go to sleep.

One-fifty-two knew how to fight. The Williams made sure so he could protect himself if the Wildmen attacked while he was on patrol. He'd never had to fight for real, but he'd practiced. He could help Jack if there was trouble.

Jack-three's footsteps faded. One-fifty-two hid the carrots next to the fence and set off after Jack, keeping to the shadows. Jack paused, standing in the middle of the street. He looked around and laughed quietly. Jack-three never laughed. The sound made One-fifty-two happy but confused.

He kept his distance and followed.

They went past the jail where the bad men went. Past the storerooms, and the outfitter. The baying of the dogs faded as they passed the stone building where the Jacks stored their weapons, then the grain silo, then the barn. The loud hum of the windmills high overhead told him where they were. The centermost point of the fortress. The vault.

One-fifty-two froze. He shouldn't be here, not near the women. His feet shuffled in place, refusing to go closer. But he was too curious to go back.

The garden was one thing, but if anyone caught him near the women without a William's permission, he'd be put in the jail. He'd be beaten, probably. He wasn't sure what happened to his kind who ventured near the women. Whispers surrounded their numbers and their bunks stayed empty until a new boy came to take their place.

Was Jack going to guard the women? One-fifty-two was sure the Williams did that. Not so much guarding, as keeping everyone else away—the Wildmen, the Jacks, the Simples. He frowned. He didn't like calling himself a Simple. He was a man, like any other. Not fat like the Williams. Not quite as solid as the Jacks, but a man.

And he had wondered what the women looked like.

He took a step forward.

His mother, he remembered her. Bits of her,

anyway. A kind smile. A hug, a soft touch to wipe away his tears, and silly songs she would sing to make him laugh. He missed laughing.

His mother had called him Joshua. He'd had a name. A name of his own before he'd become One-fifty-two. He looked at the numbers stamped on his hand.

A William had come for him, took his hand and led him to the barracks to choose a bunk of his own. It was a big step from the mattress on the floor he'd shared with five others. Then William took him aside and used a needle and ink to drive the numbers into his skin. It had hurt, but William had told him that it was part of being a man, of growing up. He'd cried, but not too loud. No one had wiped away his tears.

His mother was down below, deep within the vault. An ache filled him, to be held, to be touched. He took another step forward.

Jack-three stood at the door to the upper vault. Moths flew in spirals in the harsh light above the William who stood guard. He shook hands with Jack-three and patted him on the shoulder. Keys jangled. The William turned to the lock on the door. What William did next, One-fifty-two couldn't see. He couldn't learn this lock if he couldn't see. He'd have to get in another way.

The door opened slowly, easing as if it were very heavy. Silent, One-fifty-two crept forward, keeping to the long shadows of the barn.

William held the door open for the Jack, saying, "Enjoy your week. I'll be down to lock you in with your assigned breeder momentarily." He sorted through his keys under the light.

Jack disappeared into the vault.

An entire week with the women? With his mother? One-fifty two let out a wistful sigh.

William spun around. "Who's there?" He peered into the night.

He'd been spotted. This William would tell the others. One-fifty-two ran toward the door. "Please, I just want to see her."

"What are you doing here?"

He was so close to his mother, to the thing that would fill the ache deep inside. He would not be stopped. No one would beat him or lock him away.

"You should be in bed, Simple."

"Please."

"I said, get out of here." William reached for the gun at his side.

One-fifty-two didn't want to die. He didn't want his number to turn into a whisper. He wanted to see his mother. Wanted just a little while with her. Was that so much to ask in return for all he did for the Williams?

His mind went quiet, calm, focused. His heartbeat throbbed in his ears and strength surged through his body.

One-fifty-two swung his fist. William's head was hard like stone. He fell down like a dropped rock, too. Without a word. Just fell over.

He shook his stinging fist and stretched his fingers. He yowled as his knuckles began to smart.

And Williams said the Simples had heads like rocks? They were no better.

William didn't yell at him or try to hit him back. He didn't move at all. Maybe the William wouldn't remember who had hit him when he woke up. He'd do his best to stay away from this one tomorrow in case the William was still mad.

One-fifty-two bit his bottom lip and looked around. He couldn't see anyone, but the light from inside the vault made it hard to see very far. Jack was gone. The vault door hung open. He ducked inside and pulled it shut.

A long hallway stretched out in front of him, cement, like most everything else in the fortress. But these walls were smooth, not broken up pieces. They didn't even have cracks. He ran his fingers over the cold, gray stone.

A muffled voice in the distance caught his ear, higher-pitched than a Jack. More like a William, but yet different. He remembered voices like this. A female voice. One-fifty-two walked toward it.

The hall sloped downward, like the ramp behind his barracks where he and his friends liked to roll round rocks down to see who could go farthest. This ramp was better, though. No cracks or edges for the rocks to roll off of. They would bounce off the walls. He couldn't wait to tell his friends.

Then he remembered. He couldn't tell them. He was being naughty. Bad. Could be punished. Could be—he didn't want to think about it. With his arms wrapped across his chest and his hands clutching his shirt, he crept forward.

The voice grew louder. Then he heard another. A man. Jack-three.

The light grew softer as he left the doorway behind. It didn't hurt his eyes anymore.

He came to where the hall turned a corner and stopped, peeking around the edge. Jack stood talking to a pale girl with braided golden hair that hung to her waist.

A fluttery sensation shivered through One-fifty-two. Would she call him Joshua? He hoped she would. He wanted to hear his name from her pretty pink lips.

Jack side-stepped, blocking his view of the girl. "It's nothing personal, Arianne. I would just rather spend my time with Muriel."

"William promised me a Jack."

One-fifty-two held onto the corner and peeked a little further.

"Well, I'm sorry. There are many others. I'm sure any one of them would be happy to be with you," said Jack.

"But I'm fertile right now. If I don't produce a healthy baby by you, my record will be tarnished and the Williams will make me lie with one of what they call one of 'the few promising Simples' in hopes of some sort of miracle.

"At least the Simples are kindhearted and gentle."

Arianne stepped back, shaking her head. "I've heard Simples with other women. Believe me, they are not all gentle. Some of them bite!"

"I have a hard time believing that any William would set up a healthy woman like you with a Simple because you missed one chance at good offspring with me. We end up with enough Simples without trying to breed them. What we need are healthy children to manage them."

She sniffed. "You think I don't know that?"

One-fifty-two peeked around the corner. Was the pretty girl crying? He wanted to make her happy. Maybe he could make her laugh. He could show her that he wasn't one of the mean ones.

"Some of them really aren't all that bad. At least the ones I work with aren't." He shrugged. "They work just as hard as we do. Would it really be so terrible to give them a few nights of good memories?"

Arianne stepped away from him. Her blue eyes mere slits and her mouth hung open. It closed and then opened again. She looked like a gasping fish. Her silly face made One-fifty-two grin.

"Do you know how rare it is for us to raise our own children? We only get to keep the healthy ones. They give the Simples to the nurses and the others...they're just taken away. I want to hold my children. All of them. We only have a few years with the boys, and then they go up to the surface and we never see them again. Do you have any idea what kind of a nightmare it is to not know the fate of your own child?" She thrust her hands on her hips. Her face turned red. "Do you? Of course you don't.

You'll never bear a child. You're just a man."

Jack surged forward, jabbing his finger into her shoulder. "I have a child. A healthy child. I have the chance to find out if it's a boy or a girl and what it looks like. A chance I wouldn't normally have. Do you understand? I wasn't even supposed to know Muriel had a baby, but William had to explain so that I would agree to be with you." He pulled his finger back, his voice lowering.

Arianne bowed her head. "Oh."

If Arianne would take Jack to where they kept the babies, One-fifty-two might find his mother.

Feet shuffled on the cement floor. "If you lay with me first, I'll bring you to Muriel. But you have to promise to come back and lay with me again. Deal?"

Jack sounded happier. "Deal." He pulled her close to him, leaning down to put his lips on hers. Their faces stayed mashed together so long, One-fifty-two wondered if Arianne's tongue was stuck in Jack's mouth. Finally, they broke apart.

"William should have locked us in by now," Jack said. "He could show up anytime. We should go."

One-fifty-two stayed put for a few breaths, letting them get ahead of him as they descended deeper before he began to follow. He kept out of sight as much as he could, but the walls and occasional turn kept him at such a distance that he couldn't make out any other words between them.

Arianne seemed to really want Jack to lay down with her. Why did someone want a crowded bed?

Was she really cold? Maybe she was sad and wanted something to hold when she fell asleep like he did. He imagined Jack as a giant stuffed dog. He covered his mouth before a laugh escaped his lips. He was so close to finding his mother. He didn't want to mess up now.

CHAPTER FOUR

The lights hummed overhead, a faint buzz that hurt One-fifty-two's ears and made him feel all jittery inside. He tiptoed quiet as a rat.

Their voices grew louder. He held his breath and pressed his back against the wall.

"Who's there?" asked a girl's voice that wasn't Arianne.

One-fifty-two leapt away from the wall. He spun around, searching for the source of the voice. Then he realized that the wall wasn't a wall at all. It was a door with a rectangular, barred window at the top. A girl with wide brown eyes watched him from inside.

Maybe she was sad like Arianne and needed someone to be her stuffed dog. He puffed out his chest, trying his best to look like a Jack.

Arianne had said she didn't want to lie with a Simple. This girl might not want to either. He wasn't a Jack or a William, and pretending to be one would be lying. The Williams said lying was bad. His mother had said so, too.

"I'm Joshua."

The girl's eyebrows rose. "Is that so?" She

wrapped her thin fingers around a bar and pulled herself against the door.

He glanced down the hall but found it empty. He'd lost Jack and Arianne. Maybe this girl could take him to his mother. One-fifty-two nodded. "Can I come in?"

She scowled, looking much like a William did when he was about to beat someone. Her knuckles turned white where she grasped the bars. "You're no Jack. Get away from my damn door."

One-fifty-two shook his head, backing away. He didn't want to be her stuffed dog. "But I'm Joshua. Can you come out and help me?"

"Only if you have keys, and since you're no William, you don't have those either. You're a good for nothing Simple!" She beat on the door with her fists. "You don't belong down here alone. Get out."

William was just outside the main door. He probably had keys. If William was still sleeping, One-fifty-two could grab them. "I could let you out if you'll be nice and help me find my-"

"Nice? You want me to be nice to you?" She turned away from the door. He heard her pacing. "I'm locked up here alone, away from my sisters, waiting for a Jack that may or may not come thanks to the Wildmen. I heard about the attack, you know. A William told us so we'd be ready if we had to be."

"The Wildmen are gone. The Jacks scared them away."

"Good. Too bad the Jacks didn't scare you away while they were at it."

"Jacks don't scare me. They're nice." Williams would scare him, but they only did that when he didn't listen right or took too long to do his job.

The girl laughed. "Why would they be nice to you? You don't give them anything. You eat their food and you get in their way. I hear all about it when they visit me."

"The Williams eat way more food than I do. I don't get in their way."

"Sure you do. You waste space in the fortress. All you damned Simples. And while you're up there, bumbling about in the dirt, we're stuck down here." She slammed her hand on the door. "We should be in charge. Without us, none of you would have even been born. In your case that would have been a favor."

His breath hitched. This girl was meaner than any William. He had no doubt that if she wasn't locked behind her door, she'd be hitting him. Probably kicking him too. Girls shouldn't be mean. He'd not even done anything wrong that she should be mad at him about. She shouldn't yell at him. It wasn't her job.

Something deep inside him roared up. It made him shake, and his face felt tight, like the thing inside wanted to rip its way out of his head.

"You're the one making Simple babies. Something is wrong inside you, and that something made me wrong too." His voice, smooth and deep, surprised him. He almost sounded like a Jack, and that made him feel stronger. "It's your fault there are no Joshuas. Your fault."

The girl stared at him. "How dare you talk to me that way." She thrust her hand through the bars and waved her finger at him. "Next William I see, I'll have him beat you bloody."

One-fifty two grabbed her wrist. "No. You won't. You're going to stay here in your room forever because you're mean. You don't deserve all the pretty things me and my friends find for you."

She yanked her hand out of his grasp. "Williams give us those things, not you, stupid Simple. They give us nice things because we're important. Look at you. You've got nothing but the rags on your back."

The mean girl spun away from the door and flopped down on her big bed. She pulled a mass of blankets around her. He had never seen one person have so many blankets.

"William's don't give you nice things. We do. And the Jacks. You think Williams can scavenge in the Wilds?" One-fifty-two laughed to himself as he imagined the William who had been at the vault door trying to keep up with a Jack and four Simples as they walked for days and made their way through the broken buildings. Maybe if they still had the horse that used to pull the cart, but it had died when he was a boy. They'd yet to find another one.

"Well, if the Williams didn't tell you to give it to us, you'd keep everything for yourselves." She hugged her blankets to her chest.

Now that she'd stopped yelling, she looked more sad than angry. Maybe if he came to see her again later she'd smile and call him Joshua.

As he left her there, the shaking went away and his face felt better. The angry voice inside him curled up and went to sleep on a nice soft bed.

One-fifty-two wandered down the hall, further downward and more past doors like the mean girl's. He didn't stop to look through their bars, and he stayed quiet. If there were girls in those rooms, they didn't say anything to him. The hallway was silent, without even the familiar scurrying of rats to keep him company. But then he heard faint moaning.

Someone was hurt. He'd watched Williams fix enough cuts and aches to know what to do. He could help.

As he made another turn, the moaning grew louder and changed to gasping and grunting. Two voices. A man and a woman. They were both hurt. One-fifty-two walked faster.

Grunts and groaning grew louder and louder. One-fifty-two stopped in front of the closed door. He peered through the bars.

Arianne sat on top of Jack, bouncing on him. She didn't have any clothes on.

His cheeks burned. He tried not to look, but he kept peeking.

From all their noise, it certainly sounded like both of them were in pain, but they seemed to be having fun. Jack's hands grasped Arianne's backside, pulling her up and down on him. The rhythm got faster and faster. And then they both cried out. Arianne threw her head back. Jack's fingers dug deep into her skin, making white spots. They stayed that way, locked together, gasping, their groans changing to contented sighs.

Arianne slid off Jack and slipped under the covers beside him. "See, that wasn't so bad, was it?"

Jack shook his head and smiled. "Not at all."

One-fifty-two ducked and stepped from the door. He tiptoed away, wishing he could find a nice girl like Arianne to make him smile like Jack. He wandered further down into the vault, the air growing cooler.

Babies crying. His heart leapt. So close. He heard the mothers singing songs to the babies, their voices high and sweet. He remembered their hands on his face, ruffling his hair, smiles and kind eyes. He started to run.

Pounding footsteps echoed off the cement walls, drowning out the wailing of babies and the babbling of children. Shouts filled the air.

"Someone's coming! Something's wrong! Get the children back!" said a raspy female voice.

One-fifty-two realized the pounding footsteps were his. He skidded to a halt. "It's okay. It's just me. Nothing's wrong," he said as calm as he could manage.

The downward ramp opened into a giant room, lit from above by long rectangular white lights. He spun around, in awe of such a giant inside space. Two doors like the ones he'd passed on the way down were on the rear wall beside him. The lights were off inside. Empty.

In front of him, blocking off most of the room, were two giant doors, each far wider than he could reach with his arms stretched out. Behind the doors sat mothers with young children and babies. They all stared at him. He didn't like being stared at. He wanted to hide until they got used to him, until they stopped looking so close at every inch of him like there was something wrong, like he was someone to be afraid of. He wasn't.

But if he hid, he wouldn't find his mother. One-fifty-two stared back, trying to spot the soft brown hair he remembered tickling his cheeks. Searching for the comfortable arms that held him at night and the blue eyes that had never looked at him like these girls did.

He couldn't find her. They were all huddling together, pulling children behind them, hiding many of their faces from his view. He had to get closer, maybe even inside.

Bars ran from the floor to the ceiling. Big, thick metal handles marked where the doors came together and a heavy chain ran through them. A lock hung from the chain loop. He didn't have any keys.

He not only wanted to see his mother, he wanted to touch her. A lump formed in his throat.

"I won't hurt you. Nothing's wrong." He reached through the bars. "I just want to see my mother. Is she here? It's been so long since I've seen her. I miss her."

An old mother, her skin wrinkled so deep that he couldn't believe she was still alive, handed the baby in her arms to the mother who stood next to her. She shifted the bundle she already held to her shoulder and took the second child, balancing both.

"What are you doing here, Simple?" asked the old woman. "You don't belong in the vault."

Didn't belong? He protected them. He had been raised here. How could he not belong?

Her voice rose, scolding him like a bad child. "I said, you shouldn't be here."

"I want to see my mother."

"No one knows who your mother is, Simple. That's how the system works. Unless you had the fortune to be born to Violet, you all look pretty much the same. We haven't had a Simple with red hair in a while though." She shrugged her thin, bony shoulders.

The mother with the two babies called out, "Matron, Violet has been dead for thirty years."

"Time flies down here. Does it do that up there?"

He couldn't decide if the old woman was mad at him or curious. "I don't know."

"Of course you don't." The paper-thin skin of her face sagged. "Now then, how did you get down here? Don't bother telling me you got lost. It won't do you any good to lie to me."

"William let me in." That was mostly the truth.

She glanced over her shoulder. A couple of the other mothers got worried looks on their faces. She turned back to him. "Is that so?"

"Yes, ma'am." He remembered that the mothers

liked to be called ma'am from when he was a little boy. Maybe that would make her like him more.

She bared her yellowed teeth in what he hoped was a smile. "At least you remember your manners. See, girls? I told you what we did with these boys was worthwhile. Makes proper gentlemen out of them. Even the Simples."

"My name is Joshua, ma'am."

Her mouth dropped open just a little. "Now then, that might be a bit helpful. I thought the Williams drove your names out of your little heads when they took you from us."

He remembered the days and weeks of being called his number, of being told that his name was gone. That he'd lost it and would never have it again. But it was his name. It was the one thing he had, and no William could take that from him.

His voice sounded small, "My name is Joshua."

"I'm the Matron. That means I'm in charge here, like a William." She gave him a stern look that told him she was telling him something important. "But you can call me Grandma."

She reached through the bars and patted his arm. "It's all right, Joshua. We'll see if we can find your mother. Do you remember what she looked like?"

"She had hair like mine, and eyes like mine. And she sang nice songs to me."

Grandma's eyes grew sad, the wrinkles on her cheeks furrowing deeper. "Sounds like you had a nurse, Joshua. A nurse mother. I'm not sure she's still here. They don't live long enough to get old like me.

Let's see what we can do, though, shall we?"

Grandma kept her hand on his arm, holding him gently. It made him feel better.

"Does anyone remember a Joshua?" She looked him up and down and pursed her lips. "You look around twenty, so probably fifteen years ago or so? They take you boys so young." She tsked, shaking her head.

None of the mothers nodded. No one smiled at him. No one stood up and ran to the door to hold him. No one said his name the way he remembered his mother saying it. These mothers spoke his name with murmured voices, like he'd been bad and they all knew it.

Tears came to his eyes. "Where's my mother?"

"Come on, girls. Can someone help me out here? Joshua would like to see his mother, who looked like him," she said every word carefully, like Williams and Jacks did when they spoke to him and his friends.

The mothers looked at each other, but no one stood up.

"For heaven's sake, will someone explain it to the nurses, so one of them," she cleared her throat, "Joshua's mother will come see him?"

One-fifty-two noticed that not all the mothers were pretty like Arianne or even Grandma. Some had faces that were shaped strangely or eyes that dropped low and lips that were too big for their mouths. Their shoulders were crooked, making their dresses hang funny, and some of them were missing feet or hands or even entire legs and arms.

They looked like the things that the Williams whispered about. They were the kind of babies that the Wildmen made in their tunnels.

One-fifty-two leaned close to Grandma. She smelled like fresh, clean blankets right off the clothesline. "Why do they look like that?"

Grandma looked him in the eyes. "You really want to know, Joshua?"

Was she going to answer his question? Williams didn't do that. They told him to be quiet and not worry about things he had no business knowing. But this was Grandma, and she was nice.

He nodded.

"Because we need every woman alive, even the ones that aren't born right. You boys are different. We raise the good boys and the Simples, but the ones that aren't born right, they get taken care of."

"If you take care of them, where are they?"

Grandma glanced at the ceiling. "Up there somewhere. We give them to the Williams. Such a thing is not a job for us."

He nodded. The Williams were smart. They could fix the ones who weren't born right. "I didn't see them on the way down here."

She squeezed his arm. "No, I bet you didn't. Don't you worry about it." She sniffed. "Now, while we're waiting for your mother, why don't you tell me how you really got in here? If you're a good boy and tell me, I'll give you a cookie. Have you ever had a cookie, Joshua?"

He shook his head. He didn't remember the food from when he was little. He just remembered being hungry and then his stomach was full. Not like now. Full was just a memory. A far away one.

"William-two was sleeping by the door. I followed Jack in."

Grandma's eyes went wide. "There's a Jack in the vault?"

She glanced back at the women pointing her finger at each of them. "Three breeders are in the private rooms. Which one would William-fourteen pair a Jack with?" She took her hand from his arm and tapped her chin.

His gaze drifted to a squalling baby. The mother holding it opened her shirt and popped a big pink nipple in its mouth. He'd never seen a nipple that big before. Williams often had floppy nipples that jiggled beneath their thin shirts when they walked, but hers sat atop a skin-covered melon. He'd heard Jacks talk about nipples and breasts like they were a special treat.

One-fifty two blinked fast, trying not to stare, but his gaze kept wandering back to the bare breast. He swallowed hard. "Arianne. He's with Arianne."

"They are locked in, right?"

"The door was closed." Locked and closed meant two different things. The Jacks made sure he knew that. It was important for his patrol route. Doors had to be locked. Jiggle the handle and pull. Test. Closed was not good enough. Locked meant safe. Otherwise, the Wildmen might sneak in and kill them all in their sleep.

"Did the William lock them in?"

One-fifty-two shook his head.

Grandma clutched her hands together. "Is our door locked? Can you check for me?"

He ran his hands over the cold metal chain. The links were as thick as his little finger. The lock hung heavy at the bottom. He tugged on it. The doors shook. That reminded him of the mean girl. But she was safe, locked in her room. No one would hurt her. "Yes, ma'am, it's locked."

"Thank you, Joshua."

She might not say his name like his mother had, but she did use it and that made him warm inside.

"Could you do me a favor and go check Arianne's door? We'd all feel safer without a Jack wandering about."

"Why? Jacks keep us all safe."

"Up there," she pointed to the ceiling, "yes. But down here, Jacks lose their manners. They like women very much, you see."

"I like them too. Is that bad?"

"Not at all, my dear. But if a Jack finds his way to more than one girl at a time, he will make a mess of William-fourteen's work. We don't want to make the Williams angry. Jack needs to follow the rules like we all do. You understand, Joshua?"

Jack had made a deal with Arianne to see Muriel. He did want to break the rules. "Yes, ma'am."

"That's a good boy. Go on." She shooed him away.

One-fifty-two made his way back up the twisting hall. The way up seemed steeper. He checked the doors along the way, not sure which one was Arianne's now that he couldn't hear her and Jack. He tried not to look into the slits so he didn't make any of the girls unhappy. He didn't want to scare them. He just wanted to make sure they were safe. That would make the Williams happy with him. He was sure of it.

He tugged on door after door along the right side of the hall. Once, a voice called out, asking if there was something wrong, wondering who was there. He didn't answer. He kept walking, quick and quiet, just like he did when he was on patrol. He was good at being quiet. Quiet meant not being seen. Not being seen meant not getting shot. Jack had told him that and he remembered.

When he reached the hall where he'd come in, he started back down, checking the doors along the left side of the hall.

Locked. Locked. Locked. The knob turned. No one called out. He held his breath and then peeked through the bars. The blankets lay tossed aside on top of the empty bed. The same bed that he'd seen Arianne and Jack in. The door hadn't been locked. Jack was loose in the vault. Would he make the other girls moan like Arianne?

One-fifty-two ran back down the turning hall.

CHAPTER FIVE

One-fifty-two found Jack standing at the bottom of the vault in front of one of the long, barred doors. Arianne stood right behind him. As he descended the ramp, One-fifty-two kept to the rear wall, where he located an open door with a barred window like all the others he'd passed on the way down.

Grandma saw him and beckoned him over.

Jacks didn't like to be interrupted, and he wasn't hurting anyone. The girls were all locked up safe. Simples should wait their turn. Slipping inside the dark room, One-fifty-two watched and waited, quiet and patient.

Jack reached through the bars toward one of the women gathered at the back. "Muriel!"

Children whimpered and others pushed away from their nurses and mothers. Grandma tapped her foot and scowled. She looked to the door he hid behind.

He hadn't been able to do what she asked. She would be angry. One-fifty-two stayed in the room.

He would get out to help them if Jack started being too naughty. But the more he thought about it, how was he going to stop Jack-three from doing anything? He wasn't as big or as strong. Jacks didn't listen to orders from Simples. He'd have to find a William. But the Williams were outside the vault. If he left to find one, he wouldn't be here to help if Grandma needed him. He chewed his lip and wrung his hands.

Grandma approached Jack. "You shouldn't be here."

"You should mind your own business, old woman."

"That's Matron to you, Jack." She stood up tall and glared at him.

A mother ran toward the door with a child in her arms. "What are you doing here?" She looked at Jack and then at Arianne.

"Arianne," said Grandma. "You take that Jack back up to your room and close the door behind you. You know the rules."

Arianne rolled her eyes. "He just wanted to see Muriel." She kissed Jack on the cheek. "Remember our deal. I'll be waiting for you."

"No! You take him with you. You hear me, girl? You—" Grandma watched Arianne disappear, and again he could feel her gaze on him through the barred window.

Jack gripped the bars in his hands as if he was going to try to rip them away. "What are you doing in there, crammed all together like this?" His voice shook. "Why aren't you in your own room?"

"Muriel, get away from him."

"He's not harming anyone, Matron." She turned

back to Jack. "What do you mean? This is where we live. The private rooms are only for when we're eligible for breeding."

"But there are so many rooms, enough for all of you." He peered around her at the big room with mattresses on the floor.

There were blankets on the beds, and rugs covered most of the cement floor like One-fifty-two had seen in the mean girl's room, but this wasn't as nice and these mothers shared the room like the Simples did. Everyone shared here just like he remembered from when he was little.

"We're happy here. Now leave," Grandma said.

"How can you be happy here all crammed together like this?" Jack shook his head and pointed to the women who weren't made right. "What's wrong with them?"

Muriel turned to follow Jack's gaze. "They're nurse mothers. They help us with our children and care for the Simples."

"But they are—they—" He looked from the nurses to Muriel and back again.

"Less than perfect? Yes, but they have a purpose. Some of them are even quite smart. They're just malformed, not quality breeding stock like me." Muriel leaned in close. "Would you like to meet your daughter?"

Jack had a daughter? One-fifty-two grinned. Jack was lucky. The little girl was pretty too, just like her mother, blonde-haired with bright blue eyes and smooth white skin.

One-fifty-two wondered if he would ever have a pretty daughter. Not if he stayed here in the fortress. William-fourteen was in charge of the breeding records, and he didn't like Simples. But maybe if he helped Grandma, she would convince William-fourteen that he was good.

"This has gone on quite long enough." Grandma sputtered. "I'll see that William-fourteen hears of this. You just wait and see how long it will be before you can get with another of my girls again."

Jack leaned in close to get right in Grandma's face. "Being that the Williams need me to screw your girls, I don't think they're going to do a whole lot about it, do you?"

Grandma seemed to shrink a little. She stepped back and gathered the other mothers together, leading them away from the bars. They formed a barrier like they had when One-fifty two had first seen them, children hidden behind them. Grandma was right, Jacks forgot their manners when they were here, but still, he hadn't done anything bad.

Jack reached through the bars toward the little girl's pink cheeks. "What's her name?"

Muriel stepped back. "Nancy."

"This is stupid." He backed away and pulled two thin metal rods from his pocket. "I didn't come all the way down here to talk through bars." He slid the rods into the lock on the door and twisted them around, back and forth, swearing under his breath.

One-fifty-two grimaced. Jacks did that when they were frustrated, when they were about to turn a

Simple over to a William. He wouldn't break the lock, would he? If he tried to stop Jack, would Jack hurt him? One-fifty-two rested his hand on the edge of the door, ready to push it open if he had to.

Muriel squeaked. "Jack, what are you doing?"

"Getting you out of there."

"You can't do that." She clutched the little girl to her side. "We need to stay in here. It's safer. Jack, please, leave the lock alone."

He glanced up, his fingers holding the rods in place. "Wouldn't you like to go back to your own room where we can talk in private?"

She shook her head and backed away, taking the little girl with her. "This is my room. I have to stay here. Think of our daughter. The Williams would be so mad to find us gone. They would punish both of us. You don't want them to punish me, do you?"

"Of course not, but William-two never came down to lock me in. William-fourteen knew I wanted to see you. Maybe he passed the word along. Maybe they wanted us to have this chance to be together." He twisted the rods around again.

One-fifty-two thought his nerves might snap. He imagined rushing out to stop Jack, but every time he pictured doing so, Jack hit him. He liked Jack-three. They were friends. He didn't want Jack-three to be mad at him. Yet, he inched closer, his shoes touching the door, his fingers on the outside, creeping closer to pushing it open all the way.

"I promise I'll bring you back when we are done. I can lock you back in." The lock clicked and fell open.

One-fifty-two noticed something shining in the hands of some of the mothers. Knives. And Jack was inside their room.

Jack reached for Muriel's arm.

She dodged away.

"I'm only trying to help you." He made another grab for her arm.

Muriel ran to the huddle of mothers and handed little Nancy to one of the nurses in front.

Jack ran right behind her, grabbing the little girl. "You can't hide my daughter from me." He started for the door.

Muriel reached up under her skirt and pulled out a knife of her own. "You're not supposed to know she's yours. Give her back. You can't take her."

Jack tucked the girl under one arm and turned sideways to Muriel. "You're really going to try and cut me while I'm holding our child?"

Three other mothers broke away from the pack, all with knives in their hands. They came at Jack from both sides.

One-fifty-two leapt from the dark room and darted to the barred doors. "Jack, watch out!"

But he was too late. The woman were fast. One drove her knife into Jack's lower back, just as another wrenched Nancy from his grasp. The third sliced across his now empty arm. Muriel sunk hers deep into his stomach. Three of them slunk backward, holding their bloody knives out before them. Their arms shook and their faces were pale. The one holding Nancy retreated into the arms of the others.

Jack stood, looking down at the blood soaking through his coverall, turning the heavy, rust-colored fabric a dark burgundy. He clutched the torn fabric over his stomach. Blood seeped between his fingers.

"Jack?" One-fifty-two reached his side and gently tugged him toward the door. "We should go. You need a William to fix that."

Jack turned to look at him, blinking slowly. "One-fifty-two? What are you doing in here?"

One-fifty-two glanced at the three women still holding their knives, standing between him and Grandma who looked more angry with him than any William he'd ever seen. "We have to go."

They backed out of the room, and as soon as they were through the door, One-fifty-two closed it and looped the chain back through the handles.

Jack dropped to his knees. One-fifty-two abandoned his efforts to replace the lock.

"We have to get back outside. Hurry."

Blood dripped into the concrete floor in front of Jack and behind him. He reached into his pocket and pulled out a cloth-wrapped bundle. Holding it out in his bloody hand, he said in little more than a whisper, "I made you a present, don't you want it?"

Muriel came to the bars once again, the knife still in her hand. "I wanted you to make me safe, Jack. That's all I ever needed from you, but you failed. You're more of a danger to me than the Wildmen have ever been. You touched my daughter with your filthy hands. Who knows what germs you passed to her. You're not supposed to be in here. You could kill them all." She pointed forcefully to the children cowering behind skirts at the back of the room."

Jack looked at his dirt-stained hands. He dropped the bundle and a second later, fell to the floor beside it.

One-fifty-two shook his shoulder. "You have to get up. We have to leave."

Jack didn't answer.

"You didn't have to hurt him," he yelled at the mothers. "The Williams will punish you now. You made us all less safe. He's a good Jack." His voice came out a sad squeak, not the calm, smooth words he liked.

There was too much blood, more than he knew how to fix. He turned away from the mean mothers before they could see tears run down his cheeks. Jack needed his help.

He grabbed Jack's giant boots and dragged him to the ramp. Jack grunted and grumbled, but One-fifty-two couldn't make out the words. He had to hurry. They were leaving too much blood behind. Sweat dripped down his forehead. His muscles strained to tug the big man step by step up the ramp.

· Finally out of sight of the mothers, he stopped to catch his breath. William-four's survival lessons came back to him. The kindest William trained all the young Simples so they would come back alive from their scouting runs and scavenging trips. He heard the soft, wheezing voice of the bald William in his head. He was supposed to carry hurt people on something. He couldn't remember the word, and there weren't any sticks or branches to use here. His heart began to race as his thoughts flew. He could use blankets. One-fifty-two left Jack in the hall and ran back up the ramp until he came to Arianne's open door.

"Back already?" she said.

"I need help," said One-fifty-two.

Arianne ran to the far corner of her bedroom. "Who are you? Get out!"

He stayed in the doorway, hoping she'd be less scared. "Jack is hurt. I need a blanket."

"You hurt Jack? You animal!" Arianne reached into her skirt and pulled out a knife.

His stomach lurched. He'd seen what their knives could do. He didn't want to bleed. "Please, I need to help Jack."

She closed the distance between them in seconds, lunging at him.

Pain. He cried out. His arm hurt.

She slashed at him again. Now both arms hurt. The voice he'd heard before in his head, leapt out of his mouth in an angry roar, not even stopping to form words. One-fifty-two let the voice teach Arianne a lesson, like Williams did to Simples who refused to follow orders.

With his hand open, he slapped Arianne on the side of the head. He knew how it stung, how it made his ear buzz and his skin tingle and then burn. She staggered sideways.

If she'd just listen to him, he could get the

blanket and help Jack. She liked Jack. Why didn't she want to help him?

When Arianne looked at him, her eyes were slits and her teeth were bared like a mad dog, snarling and ready to attack.

He swung at her again. This time she spun sideways and fell against the wall with a loud crack. She slumped down to the floor. The knife fell from her hand. He grabbed it and considered taking it, but Simples weren't supposed to have knives. If a William saw him with a knife, he'd be in even bigger trouble. Instead, he slipped it under the mattress of her bed. When she got up, she wouldn't be able to hurt him or anyone else again.

One-fifty-two grabbed the top blanket off the bed. It was thick and soft. He'd never slept with a blanket so nice. It would make Jack more comfortable and easier to pull at the same time. With the blanket in hand, he ran back down to the bottom of the vault.

He could hear Grandma yelling at the girls and using Muriel's name a lot. It made him happy to know she was in trouble. They should all be in trouble. At least Grandma and the ones who had attacked Jack. He'd make sure a William knew which ones were bad.

Jack's tanned face was pale. The bloody circles on his uniform were bigger and there was a new puddle forming beneath him.

He spread the blanket beside Jack and knelt down. "Are you okay, sir?"

Jack shook his head, just a little, just enough to let One-fifty-two that he was awake.

"I'll bring you to a William. He'll fix you." He rolled Jack onto the blanket.

Jack gasped and groaned and then went silent.

One-fifty-two cringed. He didn't mean to hurt Jack more. Grabbing the front two corners of the blanket, he ran up the ramp.

By the second turn, he was walking. Jack was heavy and the ramp made his legs hurt. He'd gone up and down too many times. He hoped Arianne got up before they got back. Maybe if he stayed out of the room, she'd help Jack while he went for a William.

Sweat beaded on his forehead and his legs burned. His arms ached where Arianne had cut them. He hoped she would let him in long enough to find some bandages for his own cuts. She was the one that hurt him first, after all.

The walk up the hall seemed so much longer than the other times. Each turn brought a new level of hurt to his back. Then he saw the open door.

One-fifty-two tugged the blanket through the doorway. His breaths came in gasps as he hunched over with his hands on his legs. Sweat poured down his face and covered his body, soaking into his clothes, stinging his eyes, and making his hair stick to his face and neck.

"Arianne?" he said between gasps.

No answer.

He wiped his face on his sleeve. When he could see clearly again, he noticed Arianne still against the wall. He also noticed his sleeves were bloody and she'd cut his shirt. He'd have to wash and mend it later or William-eleven would give him extra chores for a week to earn another one.

"Help me," he said, hoping she'd answer this time.

She didn't. He crept closer to her. Blood had dried in drips down the side of her face. Her eyes were open, but they didn't watch him. She was looking at the other side of the room. One-fifty-two turned to see if she was looking at something important, but it was just a wall.

He shook her shoulder, but that only made her slip down the wall a little more. Hoping she didn't scream at him, he touched her neck where William-four had told him to feel for a heartbeat. His fingers rested on Arianne's cold skin. No beat. Dead. One-fifty-two jumped back, wiping his hand on his pants.

Jack moaned.

Leaving the dead girl were she lay, One-fifty-two ran to Jack's side. There was no one to help him. He gritted his teeth and drew a deep breath, then picked up Jack's arms and got him sitting up. He tugged and shoved until he got Jack up onto the bed.

"I'm sorry," he told Jack.

"It's okay," Jack whispered.

It didn't sound okay. It sounded like Jack was really hurt. More blood came out of the cuts and soaked into Arianne's sheets.

If the mothers were so worried about germs, they might have medicine. Williams saved the medicine for Jacks because they were important. They probably saved more for the mothers. He searched the room but didn't find the red plus William-four told him meant medicine. He tried the bathroom.

His steps echoed on the clean white tile. A white toilet and sink with only a few scratches and chips mocked him. No broken corners or deep brown stains like the ones he had to use. And a mirror. He gazed into it and decided he didn't like what he saw. He looked hollow, not quite finished, like a rough carving, missing the part that made it smooth and nice to look at.

He pulled open the drawers under the sink. Towels, thick and spongy. A toothbrush and hairbrush. Washcloths. All clean and without holes, all things he and his friends had brought back from scavenging. The women got them. Not him or his friends who sometimes got hurt exploring the old places to find these things that the Williams called treasures.

The voice rose up inside him. He didn't have time for the voice. He needed to help Jack. He slammed the drawers closed and looked on the narrow shelf over the toilet. A white box with a red plus on top sat there beside pretty bottles with colored liquid inside. He grabbed the box. One of the bottles tipped over and rolled off the shelf, crashing onto the floor. It shattered.

The room filled with a sweet stink. One-fifty-two sneezed and his eyes watered. He coughed, waving the smell away.

With the first aid kit in his hand, he made his way back to Jack. Opening the white box, he found bandages, gauze, and ointment. His mind spun, trying to remember what William-four had told him to do. Clean the wound. Yes, that was it. He held his breath and went back into the bathroom. He got the washcloths wet and grabbed the towels too.

"I'm going to clean you." He told Jack. "I need to get you out of your uniform so I can see the other cuts."

Jack's jaw tightened and his teeth clenched together as One-fifty-two unzipped the coverall and pulled it off his arms and down onto his thighs, leaving him in a thin pair of shorts. With the washcloth in hand, One-fifty-two worked his way around the cuts, washing carefully and trying not to stare at the thick muscles covering Jack's body. Sometimes he felt strong, but this was what strong looked like. Maybe, someday, if he was allowed to eat as much as the Jacks, he could look like that too.

"Just bandage them, already," Jack muttered.

Fresh blood seeped from the cuts on his back and stomach. They looked very deep. Jack's skin was cold and clammy, like a foggy morning. One-fifty-two quickly bandaged the cuts as best he could. All the blood reminded him of the bits the bears left of his friends that had wandered from their patrol paths.

One-fifty-two took a deep breath and wished away the sticky coating on his hands. "Better?"

Jack looked down and nodded. "Thanks."

One-fifty-two smiled. Jack never thanked him. He'd told him he'd done a good job before, but he would send him back out to run his patrol paths again and again. This was different. Better.

"You rest. I'll find a William." He pulled the sheet over Jack, happy to put the big man's bare chest out of sight. Each time he looked at it he thought about the hollow man in the mirror.

One-fifty-two made his way up the turning hall to the long straight stretch that led outside. The door opened. Not locked. William was still sleeping with his eyes open. Like Arianne. He shivered.

One-fifty-two knelt down and listened close. Not breathing.

He jumped up and stepped back. What had he done? Oh no. Oh no. Oh no. He shifted from foot to foot, clutching his pants in his hands over and over.

Jack needed help, but if he brought another William here, he'd see this one. Then there would be questions and Jack wouldn't get help.

He picked up William's feet. Keeping to the shadows by the barn and hoping the Jacks were busy looking outside the walls rather than in, One-fifty-two dragged the fat man back along the way he'd come, all the way to the garden. There was a new patch that some of his friends had been tilling for next season's use. No one would notice more freshly turned dirt. He grabbed a shovel from the tool shed and started to dig. When his shovel hit something at the bottom of the hole, he paused. It hadn't made a jarring clink like a rock. It was more like something soft, but harder than dirt. He dug around, determined to get whatever it was out of the way so he could get the William out of sight before he got caught.

When he finally wrestled the mass out of the soil, moonlight revealed a tiny naked body. One-fifty two jumped out of the hole and scrambled backward, stumbling and falling onto his backside in the dirt. He clamped his hands over his mouth to keep the scream inside his throat.

After a few minutes of his heart pounding like mad, he crept back over to the hole and peered in. It was definitely a baby. A boy missing an upper lip and where is front teeth would be was just a hole. And he could see another arm sticking up where he'd pried out the body. Someone was planting babies in the garden. Was this how Williams fixed the babies that Grandma said weren't born right? They killed them? His stomach turned upside down, making him dizzy until he dropped down into the dirt and lost his last meal in the hole.

He wiped his face on his torn and bloody sleeve. The moon wasn't overhead anymore. In fact, the sky wasn't all black anymore. His friends would be waking soon and coming to work. He glanced up but didn't see any Jacks nearby on the walls.

With goosebumps covering his skin, he avoided the spot with the tiny bodies and dug at the far end of the hole. The bodies smelled bad and it made him want to throw up again, but he held the bile down and dug faster until he couldn't take the smell any longer.

He scrambled out of the hole and pulled William over. The soft dirt made it very hard to pull the fat man. Black dirt clung to his pink shirt and tan pants. It looked wrong. Williams didn't get dirty.

His feet sunk deeper with each tug. After much grunting, he managed to get William to the edge of the hole. He rolled him in on top of the babies and covered them all with the pile of dirt he'd created. He spread the extra dirt around, trying to cover his footprints and the trail where he'd dragged William into the garden. No matter how many times he rubbed his eyes, he couldn't make the image of what he'd dug up go away. He shivered as he put the shovel back in the tool shed. Then he took a deep breath and ran to the closest William's house.

CHAPTER SIX

William-fourteen checked the clock. Who the hell was knocking at his door at 5 a.m.?

"This better be important!" He shoved his blankets aside and rolled out of bed. His robe hung on the hook. He pulled it on and made his way to the door.

The knock sounded again.

"I'm coming!"

He undid the locks, all except for the heavy chain, and peeked through the two-inch gap. A damned Simple, covered in dirt, stood there wringing his dark-stained hands and staring at the ground.

"Well, what is it?"

The Simple glanced up at him and then back at the ground. "A Jack, sir. He's hurt."

"That so?" The damned Jacks were always getting into trouble. Too much testosterone in their systems. If he didn't need them all for breeding, he'd put the worst of them down.

"And where is this Jack?" He undid the chain and opened the door a bit further. The stench of sweat wafted in.

"In the vault, sir."

"Jack-three was in the vault. How did he get word to you if he was inside?"

The Simple whispered, "I followed him in."

William scowled. This was going to require getting dressed and starting his day several hours ahead of schedule. "Where was the William on duty at the door?"

"He was right there, by the door."

Simples knew better than to lie. This one didn't appear to be, but something was definitely off. "Hold on, let me get dressed."

"Jack's hurt. Please hurry."

William left the door open a crack. He took a pair of tan pants from the chest at the foot of his bed and pulled them on. "Why don't you tell me how Jack-three came to be hurt in the vault?"

"Mean mothers stabbed him."

The women were allowed knives for their own protection in case the Wildmen ever made it into the vault. They'd never used their knives to his knowledge, but it seemed arming the female populace had been a wise move after all. Losing even a single one of them would be tragic.

But how did Jack manage to get access to more than one? The doors were kept locked except for the designated breeder. Even at that, a William would have followed the Jack in and locked the pair inside her room. Perhaps that's how he missed the Simple walking in.

"Do you mean one woman stabbed him?" he called out.

"No. Lots of mean women. I used the first aid kit like William-four taught us." He smiled proudly.

"And just where was Jack when he was stabbed?"

The Simple shuffled his feet. "He was down at the bottom of the vault."

William yanked a yellow shirt over his round shoulders and worked on the buttons. Jacks weren't allowed to see the bottom of the vault. It would do no one any good if a testosterone-crazed Jack got wind of just how many women there were and that he could somehow attain access to a large number of them instead of just one. If they were raped, there'd be chaos with the women and with the plans Isaiah had laid out before his death.

The old man hadn't been successful with breeding more Isaiahs until shortly before he'd died. It would be years before the three and six-year-olds were ready to take his place. They couldn't afford to screw up the breeding records now.

"Bring me to Jack-three." William locked the door before following the Simple to the vault.

Alarm spread through William when he saw the empty seat next to the door. There was no sign of the William that had been on duty. The Simple stared at the empty chair too.

"He was here when you left, wasn't he?" The Simple seemed to ponder the question for a moment, then he nodded.

The door to the vault hung open. Maybe William was inside helping the Jack. He hoped that was the case.

He went in. The Simple followed close behind, but slowly overtook him and then led the way.

William hated the vault. The hallways were so long and the steep slope made his legs hurt.

The Simple stopped in front of a door. "He's in there."

William reached for his keys.

"Not locked." The Simple pushed the door open but didn't go in.

William opened the door the rest of the way and stepped inside. Jack-three lay on the bed.

Blood had soaked through the bandage on his stomach. The bandage on his arm was still clean. His pale skin was clammy. William pressed his fingers on the man's thick neck. He still had a pulse. Maybe he'd make it. For now, he needed to make sure the women and children were safe.

"Stay with him. I'll be back." He left the Simple standing at the door and made his way down the ramp to the bottom of the vault. By the time he caught sight of the double doors, sweat ran down his temples. Would it have been so difficult for his ancestors to have chosen a sprawling research facility to make their central stronghold rather than a deep one?

A bloody trail led from the double doors, up the middle of the hall and around the corner where he'd come. The women stood as he approached their door.

"What happened here?" The chains were woven

through both door handles, but the lock lay on the floor. He picked it up and examined it. It was as solid as ever.

The Matron stepped forward, protecting her flock as usual. "The Jack picked the lock. Your William stationed at the door is sorely lacking in his duties. That Jack should have been locked up with his assigned breeder. He should have never made his way down here." Her skeletal hands shook and her wrinkle-encased eyes narrowed as she glared at him.

"I assure you, I'm looking into it. Was anyone hurt?" The women looked fine. A couple of the nurse mothers sat on the floor in out of the way places and rocked themselves, but most went about their duties, caring for the Simple children they'd been assigned.

"We won't know until time passes. He touched one of the children."

William sighed. "I've told you before, you're breathing the same air down here as we do up there. Those of us left are immune to the virus."

"You can't prove that. We haven't been out there in generations. You don't know what would happen to us."

"Matron, you're down here for your safety, not from germs, but from men."

"That's not what Isaiah said. There are air cleaners." She pointed to the ceiling. "They protect us."

He shook his head, wondering what games the old man had been playing. "And what about the

Jacks, and all of us who bring you food and everything else you have here? What about me, now?"

The Matron looked him up and down. "You're cleaned, but that Jack wasn't. There are procedures in place. Isaiah told me all about them. Decontamination rooms. You think that just because we live down here, we're ignorant?"

William had seen the decontamination rooms. They were covered in dust and cobwebs, their seals had been broken long before his birth. The manpower and supplies were in short supply. They'd stopped using the rooms long ago. The doors and seals had been dismantled and cleared away soon after he'd begun to assist Isaiah in order to make entering the vault easier. The old procedures were nothing more than a fading memory.

But if memories kept the Matron happy, and Isaiah hadn't enlightened her as to the truth, he would just smile and nod. "I wasn't aware Isaiah had kept you so well informed."

"I know more than you think." She leaned closer to the bars, closer to him. "We were attacked, and this wasn't even from Wildmen. This was one of our own. One that should have been protecting us!"

"What did the Jack want with you?"

"He was trying to abduct Muriel and their child. How did he even know he'd fathered a child? Jacks aren't to be trusted with that information. We give them nothing but something to smile about. They own nothing and no one. We have a policy."

A policy the Matron and the Isaiah had strictly enforced. Isaiah had been a secretive man, quiet and withdrawn. He even ate alone, preferring his books and records to human company. Far too solitary for William's comfort. It was too much time alone that inspired things like Isaiah's surrogate program. Granted it was the only reason they now had young Isaiahs, but it was too much science. From what he could tell, science was what got them all into this mess to begin with.

"I said I'd check into it. There will be a thorough investigation. Not to fear." He slipped the lock back into place and clicked it shut. "It won't happen again."

"What's to stop it from happening again? He picked the lock, William. Are you teaching Jacks lock picking?"

"Of course not."

"Then where did he learn it?"

"I said I'd look into it." He'd read a book most likely. Jacks would have access to them when out on scavenging duties. With the shortage of able-minded children growing more extreme over the years, there weren't enough Williams around to make sure that everything was in order, let alone to go out into the wilds for weeks at a time. They needed to lean on the Jacks now and then.

One of the nurse mothers came forward, beckoning to the Matron. "Need help," she said in a guttural voice.

The Matron nodded and waved her away. "You

take care of this, William, or we'll all be sorry. You hear me?"

He put on his most placating smile. "I will. Don't worry."

"Oh save it, you impotent ball of fat. I'm no Simple. This is about reviving humanity, not about getting me to stop nagging you." She pointed him up the ramp. "Go."

William swore under his breath. It was bad enough knowing he was of no help whatsoever to creating the next generation. He didn't need it shoved in his face. It wasn't his fault that Williams were born that way.

He shot a glare at the Matron. "Take care of the others. The fate of humanity rests in your hands."

"Thank God it doesn't rest in yours," she said.

William left her standing there. Better to leave before he lost any more face. He just hoped the other women hadn't overheard them.

He mumbled to himself all the way up the ramp and into Arianne's room. Damned woman. If the Matron wasn't so important to the others, he'd have her removed and turned into fertilizer for the garden like all the other discarded bodies. Between the Matron, the Jack bleeding all over Arianne's bed, the missing William, and the idiot Simple who was now gazing at him as if he expected him to work a miracle, he wasn't sure which was the cause of his sudden headache. He cursed them all and plopped down on to the bed beside Jack-three to catch his breath.

The Simple said, "Can you fix Jack?"

"I'm not a doctor. None of us are." William ran his hands through his short, sweat-soaked hair. One should not have this much exercise this early in the morning.

They hadn't had real doctors in over seventy years. Only medical journals remained. Any illness could turn deadly and most did. Stitches, he could manage. The women took care of birthing the babies. That was their work. He wanted no part of it.

Isaiah had taken care of implanting the surrogate nurse mothers. In his last days, he'd instructed the Matron how to continue the process, but the last of the stored sperm had been ruined when they'd lost two of the wind-powered generators to the lack repair skills and replacement parts. What remained of the medical equipment now sat gathering dust, their plugs still inserted into dead outlets. The little power that remained kept the lights on in the vault. He dreaded the day they lost those. The Matron would have a lot to say about that.

When he'd finally caught his breath, he said, "We need to take him up top to see if we can save him."

Their population dwindled with every year. Each year fewer viable breeders were born. Fewer Jacks. More Williams. More Simples.

"Carry him."

The Simple's shoulders slumped. "I can't, sir. I'm too tired."

"Well, I can't carry him. How did you get him

this far?"

"Carried him on a blanket, sir."

"Then do that again."

The Simple glanced out the door and back at William. Perhaps this one wasn't as stupid as some of the rest.

"We're halfway to the outside door. It's not that far."

"I'll need to get him off the bed, sir."

"Of course you will." Did the Simple think *he* was stupid? Good Lord, humanity really was ending.

The Simple rubbed his hands together and went to the end of the bed. "I'll get these blankets on the floor." He stood there as if waiting for something.

"Well?"

"Would you like to wait outside?"

"Why?"

The Simple's gaze darted around the room and his red-stained hands clenched and unclenched on his ill-fitting pants.

"What is on your hands?"

"Jack's blood."

His filthy and torn shirt sleeves were two inches too short on his long arms. Mismatched shoes covered his big feet. He had the frame of a Jack, but he'd gone wrong in the womb, leaving him nothing but a slow, dirty excuse for a young man.

"What were you doing earlier? Crawling through the gardens?"

"No." The Simple gazed at the floor.

"Get the blankets. I'll help you lift him off the

bed."

"Yes, sir." He pulled off two blankets that were draped over the end of the bed and spread them on the floor.

William caught sight of a head of hair and pale skin. "Arianne?"

The girl didn't answer.

He went over to her.

Dried blood covered the side of her face, matting the hair that rested on her shoulder and trailing down her dress.

"What have you done?" His voice shook. He felt her neck. Dead. Their best breeder, dead. Dread took hold of him. "Did Jack kill her or you? What happened here?"

The Simple backed away. He shook his head but didn't utter a word.

Simples didn't lie. Not out loud anyway and certainly not to a William. "What is your number?"

"One-fifty-two," he whispered.

"You'll be going to jail, One-fifty-two. What do you think about that?" He stalked toward the cowed Simple.

"I don't want to go to jail." He shook from head to toe.

"Did you do something to the other William, One-fifty-two?"

The Simple backed up farther until his back hit the wall.

"One-fifty-two, how do you feel about execution? Are you aware how perilous our situation is here? Do you have any idea how much we need every able-bodied member of our population? You've killed a William. You've killed a breeder. There are hundreds of you, but only a few of us. You are expendable, One-fifty-two. Do you have any idea what that means?"

"No?" his voice sounded tiny, like a small child.

"It means no one will miss you, you stupid malfunction of nature. You are a dead end. A defect. A waste of air! And you killed two of the people we needed most! How could you? Why?" He realized his fists were clenched and a degree of anger he'd never felt before coursed through him.

Gone was the familiar voice of reason, the never-ending patience, the need to keep peace between all parts of his society. He wanted this man dead. Right now.

But he needed the Simple if the Jack could be saved. Perhaps the rest of the Simple's story wasn't quite correct either. Did the Simple have more of a part in Jack getting into the women's room? If he killed the William at the door, he could have grabbed his keys. This picking the lock story could be discounted. But the Matron had seemed outraged. Maybe they were both to blame, the Jack and the Simple. He wouldn't know until he could speak to the Jack.

"You will put this man on the blanket and you will carry him to the jail, where I will lock both of you up until I get this mess all sorted out."

"But Jack needs help," the Simple said.

"You know what they used to call you? Syndromes and Spectrums. Special, they said. Touched in the head. They kept you locked away and medicated so you wouldn't hurt yourselves or others." He pointed to Arianne. "You see why? This is what happens. You're all broken inside." He slapped One-fifty-two upside the head. "It's not fair that most of you were immune." His heart beat faster, racing until it felt as though it might burst right out of his chest. He covered it with his hand as if he could hide the frantic beating inside. Slowly, the pressure on his heart eased.

"You were a burden to society then, and you still are now. Worthless. A waste of our precious resources."

The Simple watched him, his head tilted like a dog listening for prey.

"What are you looking at? Move!"

The Simple stared at the ground, looking like he'd rather be cowering in the corner. "Yes, sir."

He spread the blankets on the floor and took the Jack's shoulders while William took his legs. They lifted him down to the floor. The big man groaned but didn't open his eyes.

"Bring him up." William looked at Arianne one last time. A pretty girl, mother to two young Jacks, and the daughter of the last line to naturally bear an Isaiah. Such hope for the girl and now she was nothing more than fertilizer. He'd have to send another William down to bring her out later. He couldn't let the other women smell a corpse. He needed time to figure out what to tell the Matron.

Each step up the ramp made his legs burn. His breath came in gasps and sweat soaked his clothes.

The survivors hadn't been so concerned with that sort of thing when they'd used the vault to house their computers and top minds, hoping to save them from the death above ground. It didn't work. They'd all died anyway. Even the computers had long since died, victims to surges of power and viruses.

He shook his head. Everything had fallen to viruses—dogs, cats and other domestics. A few survived, breeding resistant bloodlines, but they didn't come close to filling the barn inside the fortress. Simples tended to the chickens, the pigs, sheep and the few cows that lived to adulthood.

They trudged up the turning ramp. The Simple ambled along, pulling the Jack behind him and yet still staying well ahead. Damned Simples shouldn't be better off than Williams. He should have been given the able body instead of the wheezing one that wanted nothing more than a chair in which to plant itself right then. He cursed his lack of forethought to have sought out one of the Williams who were more accustomed to traveling within the vault.

A droplet of sweat dripped from his upper lip into his gasping mouth. Disgusted, he clamped his mouth shut, but his nose couldn't take in all his body demanded. Seconds later he admitted defeat, wiped his wet sleeve over his face and panted as he fought to catch up to the Simple.

The smell of dirt and damp morning air drifted

toward them. The sun was over the horizon in its full glory when they emerged from the artificial light of the vault. He shaded his eyes and went through his keys, locking the vault door behind him.

"That way." He pointed the Simple toward the jail's rugged walls, just visible across the yard.

The Simple trudged forward, dragging the Jack through the dirt behind him. For a moment William felt bad, knowing the injured man had pebbles in his back, but only for a moment. He'd threatened the women. He didn't deserve sympathy.

Dogs barking in the kennel told him he'd missed breakfast. The dogs were getting theirs. Someone else had eaten his portion by now. Probably some damned Simple from the way his luck was going this morning. He'd have to dig into his personal stores hidden under his bed when he got back.

Dew glistened on the scattered patches of grass alongside the pathway. They passed the chicken shed. Chickens gathered within the low fence around their home, scratching at the dirt and casting annoyed looks at the Simple on duty who was searching for their eggs.

One-fifty-two grunted and tugged at the blanket, his stride growing slower and his body at more of a forward incline than it had been even when they marched up the ramp inside the vault.

The more worn out the Simple was, the less of a threat he'd be. Simples crumbled under the authority of Williams anyway. That was ingrained in them as soon as they were brought up from the vault as children. When he'd accused this one, he'd been no different than the rest, submissive to the core. He'd be willing to do anything to gain a pat on the head or a smile.

He'd use that trait to get to the bottom of what had gone wrong with One-fifty-two, and he'd make sure that mishap didn't occur with any of the others. Then the boy would end up in the garden with the rest. His mouth watered at the thought of the crop of crisp carrots that were due to be harvested today. At this rate, they'd have a good crop next year, too.

They passed the long row of sections of cement stairs that had once led into homes but now led to nothing. Some still had iron railings embedded in them. Some only had twisted stumps where the railings had been harvested for use as spikes on the fortress walls. Thick blocks placed in long hollow rectangles poked through the weeds, outlining where buildings had once stood. Their bricks now formed the base for the walls that protected the fortress from the Wildmen and the animals that had survived.

Bears, in particular, had remained quite hardy. The Jacks had managed to shoot a few, but the large beasts were wary of coming too close to the fortress and often chased down the Simples who left their assigned patrol path. Stupid Simples. If they kept to the well-worn paths close to the walls, they'd be fine.

The least the idiots could do would be to undress first. Clothing ran in short supply these days and what little the Simples wove was of far less quality. They needed all they could salvage or they'd be reduced to wearing furs and tanned hides within a couple generations. Back to being cavemen.

William trudged along the path. His chest begged for him to take a break. Just a little farther and he could sit down without admitting he was sorely out of shape, embarrassingly so compared to a half-starved Simple pulling a two-hundred-some pound, muscle-covered Jack for the second time that morning.

At least Jacks respected Williams for their knowledge of Isaiah's plans. The Simples had no grasp of that sort of thing. Williams had to maintain absolute authority over them at all times. The last thing they needed was for the Simples to realize that all they needed to do was run fast or keep a William on his feet for more than half an hour and they could be easily overpowered. There would be chaos. A world run by Simples. What a nightmare.

He straightened himself and did his best to hide his huffing and puffing. If the Simple turned around, William would not be seen as weak.

Keeping Simples underfed, especially failed Jacks like One-fifty-two, was a line of defense. The tall, gangly men occasionally exhibited disturbing moments of clarity and their labors kept them strong. While it made them more useful than others, it also made them more dangerous. If only the bears had taken this one before he'd done harm.

A shadow moved along the ground. William glanced up to see a Jack walking atop the wall. He didn't relish having to inform the Jacks that their numbers might be one less very soon. They were a close brotherhood and would not take his loss well. Angry Jacks were to be avoided. He'd wait to call one down to deal with the Simple until he'd gotten the information he needed.

A gentle breeze wound its way through a cornfield surrounded by the remnants of an oval of cement walkway. Two generations of William's ago there had been fields of corn outside the fortress walls. Jacks had kept an eye on corn and wheat and sprawling tangles of melon vines. But the Wildmen raided those same fields, like drawing in rats with crumbs. They couldn't afford rats so close to the women. They'd burned the fields with the Wildmen in them and made do with the available space within the walls.

Making do was what the Williams were good at. The leaves rubbed together, calming him with their soft sounds of rightness. The animals would eat. The people would eat. All would be well.

William pulled the ring of keys from his pocket. His fingers ran over their worn metal ridges, searching for the correct key. Not the round ends, not the square ends, not the two skeleton keys that he didn't even know what they went to but didn't dare discard. At last, his fingertips rested on the oblong end of the gold-toned key that fit the jail lock. He rubbed his thumb over it, secure in the knowledge that this key kept them all safe.

The urge to revise the standards of validity for the young Simples came upon him as he watched

One-fifty-two tug the Jack up to the door of the jail. They couldn't afford losses like this again. He'd talk with the other Williams and then pull the Jack-like Simple toddlers out for extermination. The nurse mothers wouldn't miss a few boys and they'd all be safer for it.

His mind raced through excuses to give the Matron, something she could use to pacify her charges if they asked questions. Food rations. Yes, that would work. He and the Williams already had that groundwork in place to maintain control above. Why shouldn't it also help them below?

When the Isaiahs came of age, any resources they had available to them would mean a better chance at survival for them all. Until then, the fortress was under an unspoken cutback of everything. Between some creative lies to the Jacks and some misleading of the Simples, the Williams had been able to store extra supplies away for the past few years. When the Isaiahs were ready to take up the quest of putting humanity together again, they would have a stocked fortress at their disposal.

He slipped the key into the lock and turned it. The lock clicked. He turned the knob and the door swung open. "Bring him inside."

The Simple gulped. Sweat ran down his face and neck. His filthy shirt was plastered to his body. He nodded and pulled the Jack inside.

"Here to bring me food?" a hopeful voice called out.

William scowled. Wildmen were worse than

Simples. Diseased, contaminated, and nothing but a body waiting for the inevitable: extermination.

"Why bother? We've got the information we need from you." Most of it anyway. The damned man had been less forthcoming than the interrogating William would have liked. Not that he felt up to taking a try at the wounded man himself at the moment. William just wanted to sit down with a cold glass of water and rest. Maybe a nap. A nap sounded like exactly what he needed. His arm tingled as he put the key back into his pocket. He had definitely overdone it with the walk up the ramp and then losing his temper with the Simple.

"Put him in the cell across from the Wildman and lock the door. I'm going to go fill out the log book." He waited until the Simple had made his lurching way to the cell before stepping around the corner and taking a seat at the desk there. The chair was too small and too hard, but at least he was sitting.

Dizziness washed over him, blurring the names in the book. He made a show of turning the crinkly pages in case the Simple returned before he'd recovered. Blinking, he tried to focus on the names as he flipped back through the book. Williams, Jacks and numbered Simples gave way to names he'd never put to faces, even women's names. He wondered what the fortress must have been like with such a diverse population, with enough men and women that no guilty person was safe from ending up in a cell.

Still feeling faint, he let go of the book and dropped his swimming head into his hands. He needed fresh air. Yes, fresh air would help. But the pins and needles in his arm grew worse and the dizziness refused to ease. Pain blossomed in his chest, much more than the discomfort he'd felt on the walk here.

What was the name of the damned Simple? He needed some water, someone to help him get outside, someone to run and fetch another William. "Simple!"

A cell door clanged shut. Footsteps came closer.

"Simple!" He gasped, unable to take a deep enough breath to satisfy his lungs.

A homely face peered around the corner, staring at him like it was completely ordinary that he should be yelling and gasping and clutching his chest.

"Go get another William! I need help!"

The Simple just stood there, his thick lips drawn into a straight line.

"Do something! Go!" The room lost focus around the edges. The Simple finally stepped toward him, but instead of turning toward the door, he came closer.

"I'm having a heart attack, for God's sake." He'd read about enough heart attacks to know that was what he was feeling, but knowing did nothing to stop it.

He reached for the Simple but only managed to topple from the chair onto the floor. "Get help!" The edges thickened, taking more of the room with them as they melted into blackness. "I'm dying!"

The Simple nodded.

Panic overtook William. His chest hurt so bad. No one would get here in time to help him, and it was all this Simple's fault! If the damned Simple hadn't woke him up so damned early and led him down the damned ramp, got him all riled up and then made him walk back up and out again, he'd be digesting a big breakfast in the comfort of his own house and pondering the breeding schedule. But no, he was sitting here dying in front of an idiot, a mostly dead Jack, and a lame Wildman.

His mind finally found what it had been searching for. "One-fifty-two, that's your name. Go get help!"

The Simple knelt down beside him, his eyes far more intent than any Simple's had the right to be. "No, my name is Joshua."

William opened his mouth but nothing came out and nothing went in. The room shrank to a pinpoint of light.

CHAPTER SEVEN

Phillip heard the boy sobbing around the corner. The William has been silent for a while. The irritating fat man must have died. No one would miss him. There always were a few too many Williams for anyone's taste. No one needed to be bossed around like that. They might as well be sitting on a throne, frowning at their subjects and dispensing orders.

"Joshua, is it? Why don't you come over here, boy, and tell me what's got you so sad."

The sobbing turned into a sniffle and then stopped. The boy peeked around the corner. "I didn't kill him."

"Wouldn't have blamed you if you had." Would have praised him for it actually, but it wouldn't do him any good to tell the boy that. "I know you didn't kill him."

"The other Williams will think I did. Arianne is dead and the William at the door." He sniffed again.

"You've been busy." Phillip shifted on the floor, trying to find a more comfortable position. The damned Jack who'd shot him lay in the cell across the way. He didn't look so good and Phillip didn't feel real bad about that either. In fact, if Joshua wanted to add that man to his list of murder victims, he might do a little jig if his feet ever healed.

The boy blinked. His eyes filled with tears. "I didn't mean to kill anyone."

"I'm sure it was all an accident." But would the others in the fortress see it that way? Phillip stifled a grin. "Did this William know you'd hurt the others?"

Joshua nodded, dropping his gaze to the floor.

"Well then, what did he think about that?" Phillip pulled himself closer to the bars.

"He said," Joshua swallowed hard, "he said that I was going to be killed."

"How about we don't let that happen, hmm?" He wrapped his hands around the rough metal of the bars. "I'll tell you what. I'll help you if you help me. Sound like a deal?"

Joshua cocked his head and seemed to ponder his proposal.

"You go to the William over there and get his keys for me, and I'll help you get out of here alive."

Joshua pointed at Phillip's feet. "You can't walk."

"But I'm a hell of a lot lighter than that Jack there. I bet you're strong enough to carry me. What do you say?"

"I'm tired. I really don't want to carry anyone anymore."

"And my feet hurt like hell, boy. Sometimes we just gotta buck up and do what needs to be done."

Joshua slumped against the wall behind him and

stood there, staring at his shoes.

"We don't have all day, boy. Come on. You don't want a William wandering in here and finding you, do you?"

"William can't talk now. He's dead."

"Think about it, Joshua." Phillip's fingers clutched the bars with all the intensity of his hope. "There you are, standing free against the wall. William is over there, dead. Jack looks about ready to kick the bucket any minute. Who will they think killed them? I'm in here, locked up. That would leave you, my boy. Just you."

Joshua sucked on his lower lip, glancing between Jack and the desk around the corner. "I don't want to die."

"No one does. Now go get those keys, and we'll get out of here."

"Okay." Joshua disappeared around the corner. Fabric rustled.

"The keys should be on a ring, probably in a pocket somewhere or on his belt."

Come on, he urged silently. This boy was so much better than the poor men he was used to, more aware, more capable. Perhaps not quite all there in the head, but he knew the Williams didn't exactly endorse educating their minions. With a little time and encouragement, Joshua could be a valuable member of his tribe. And he had keys.

"Joshua, those keys, did you find them yet?"

Clinking metal answered his question before the boy did. "Yes."

"Good boy, can you bring them here, please?"

Joshua reappeared with a thick ring of keys in his hand. "I will get in trouble if I give you the keys."

Phillip rolled his eyes. "You are in trouble, Joshua. Did you forget that you killed people?" He ran a hand over his face and took a deep breath. "But you're not in trouble with me. I can make sure you're safe and bring you to my home."

Joshua backed away. "But this is my home."

"It will be your grave if you stay. If you let me out, I'll see that you get some food and make new friends. Friends that will call you Joshua."

"I'd like that." The boy came over to the cell door, but he still looked uncertain. "But I shouldn't give you the keys."

"How about you keep the keys then and just unlock the door?"

"Okay." He held up the key ring and looked over each key. "Which one?"

"I don't know. Try them all."

Joshua nodded, and brow scrunched with determination, set about his task of matching the right key to the lock.

Phillip kept his eyes on the outside door, as if by the sheer force of willing it to remain closed, he could ensure his freedom.

"What about Jack?" asked Joshua.

"What about him?"

"Can I unlock his door too?"

"Let's not worry about Jack right now. Concentrate on this door first."

The boy nodded and tried several more keys to no avail. "But Jack is my friend."

Phillip glanced at the big man on the floor. His bare chest was still. "Jack is already free. Don't worry about him."

Joshua halted his key search and turned around. "He's still locked up. He's not free. I'm not stupid."

"Of course you're not. I mean to say, he's dead."

Joshua sank to the ground as if his legs had melted beneath him. "I didn't hurt Jack. I didn't. I didn't."

It clearly wasn't a good time to ask, but he was curious. "Who did?"

"The mean mothers." Tears ran down Joshua's face. He slid across the hall on his backside and fumbled with the keys.

"What are you doing? We need to get out of here." Phillip wished his feet didn't hurt so bad so that he could stand. If he were standing, he'd feel less helpless.

"Shut up." Joshua glared at him through his tears. "I worked hard to get Jack here so William could make him better. I pulled him and pulled him. I walked and tugged. I tried so hard." He picked one key and slid it into the lock. It clicked.

Sure, now he gets lucky. Phillip beat the heels of his hands against his forehead. He wanted to scream, I don't give a rat's ass about this Jack. But that wouldn't make Joshua any more agreeable. "What do you think unlocking his door will do for him now? We need to get out of here."

Joshua shook his head and swung Jack's door open. "Jack is my friend." He crawled inside and sat next to the dead man.

"Jack is dead."

"No." Joshua wrapped the blankets around Jack, tucking him in as if he could be more comfortable. "He can see me."

"What?"

"His eyes are open. He can see me." Joshua patted Jack's shoulder. "It will be okay, Jack. William will make you better."

"William is dead."

Joshua nodded. "There are other Williams."

"There are other Jacks too. Do you think they will be happy to find you alone with one of their dead? They'll think you killed him, and they'll be mad."

"No." The boy drew his legs up against his chest and wrapped his arms around them, resting his chin on his knees. "Jack is my friend."

"I bet Jack didn't even know your name. Did he ever use your name, Joshua? Did he?"

Joshua wiped at the tears on his cheek. Another flood of them rained down. "No," he whispered.

"Friends know their friends' names, Joshua."

The boy cried harder, rocking back and forth.

Phillip closed his eyes and took a deep breath. "If you unlock my door, I'll fix Jack. Would you like that?"

The boy's rocking continued. "You can fix him?"

"I'll see what I can do, but I can't try unless I can get over to him. You have to unlock the door."

"Okay." Joshua got to his feet and flipped through the keys again, trying one after another.

Phillip swore, his heart beating faster and faster. "Try that same one that opened Jack's lock."

Joshua flipped back to the key and slipped it into the lock. It fell open.

"Thank God." He let out a huge sigh. "Now, help me over there."

Joshua reached down and grabbed Phillip's upraised arms. The boy hauled him to his feet. He gasped and cried out as Joshua half-dragged him over to Jack's cell and plopped him down. He stood there with his arms folded across his chest. "Fix Jack."

Phillip pressed his fingers against Jack's neck. Nothing. His skin was already cooling. Good riddance. He slid his hand over Jack's broad face, closing his eyes.

"There, that's the best I can do. He can't see you anymore. We can go."

Joshua looked down at Jack and Phillip. "I didn't hurt him," he said in a tiny voice.

"I know. Come on."

"Wait." Joshua knelt down next to Jack and pulled the blankets and top half of the coverall aside. He searched around in the pockets on the legs.

"What are you looking for?" Maybe the Jack had a weapon on him.

"A present."

"For who?" Not that he had anything against

scavenging off the dead, that was a necessity these days, but they didn't have time for it.

"A girl."

"What girl?"

"A nice one. Jack made a present for his Muriel, but she was mean. If you have nice girls, I might find one to give it to."

"Hurry up then, and bring the keys."

Joshua pulled out a little bundle of cloth. He beamed a triumphant smile and shoved the package into his own pants pocket. "Where are we going?"

"Away from here, where we'll be safe from Jacks and Williams."

"But Jacks have guns. They won't let us leave."

"Jacks use Simples to run the patrol paths."

Joshua nodded.

"Then let's go do your job."

"You can't do my job, you can't run."

"We're not actually going to do your job." He had to remember who he was speaking to. "I meant we can leave by pretending we are going to do your job."

"Oh." Joshua picked Phillip up and stood him against the wall. "You walk. I'm tired."

"I can't walk, you—" he caught himself before he sealed his fate. "I need help. You have the keys right?"

"Yes." Joshua patted his bulging shirt pocket.

"Good. Now back up so I can hold on to your shoulders. You're going to have to carry me until we get to my people."

Joshua backed up and then held Phillip's arms. He clasped his hands around the boy's chest.

"You're not very heavy," said Joshua.

"Benefits of not having much food, I guess."

"But you have food for me, right?"

Phillip grimaced. "Yes."

Joshua headed for the door. "Do you have cookies?"

"Maybe." What the hell were cookies? "We'll have to see when we get there."

The boy opened the door and looked both ways. "Do you have nice girls?"

"Yes." His women weren't spoiled queens like these ones were. But these ones were healthy. "Joshua, those keys, will they open the vault?"

"I think so."

Phillip grinned through his pain. Maybe this raid wouldn't be for nothing after all. "How many men guard the door?" If this boy wasn't afraid of killing people, they might be able to get in and take a few of the women with them.

"None. I buried that William in the garden."

"You're kidding." Could his luck get any better? Well, other than getting shot and not being able to walk...

Joshua shook his head. "It is bad to tell jokes. Williams might think it is a lie. Liars get punished."

"No one likes to get punished. How about we head to the vault before we leave?"

"No." Joshua came to a halt. "No vault. Those women are mean."

"I bet they won't be mean if we tell them they can come out and see the sky."

Joshua gazed upward. "The mean girl said she wanted to see the sky but the others were scared of it. I don't know if it would make them happy."

"I bet it would. Do you remember where the vault is?"

The boy nodded.

"Good. Let's go." He held on tight as Joshua hunched over and scuttled down the path.

Simples worked in the fields but they were focused on their tasks. The Jacks on the walls looked outward rather than in. The one William he did see sat in a chair next to a garden plot supervising two Simples with his nose deep in a book. Hugging Joshua's back and tucking his head low, they finally came to what appeared to be the center of the fortress. The heart that they'd tried for generations to make it to, and now he would be the one. Phillip grinned.

The concrete building stood before them, the late morning light shining off the long, narrow stripes of windows that dotted the wall. He peered into the windows as they ran by, but the glass was darkly tinted and he couldn't see a thing beyond his own reflection. He looked away, not wanting to see the truth of his years. He preferred the pleasant memory of his youthful face smiling back at him in the stream that ran outside their tunnels. He'd been barely a man then, just back from his first raid on the fortress. Back when he'd considered victory the act of taking down a Jack, or a William, or even a few Simples without losing any of his own men. Each fortress-dweller they got rid of meant one less defender the next time around. But they kept breeding, and at a faster and more successful rate than his tribe.

Those types of successes were no longer victories and each defeat cut deeper. The last effort had cost them dearly, losing vast numbers of their poor men—who would not even be considered Simples by the standards of the Williams. But they were men and the tribe would miss them. It had been a hard decision to sacrifice them, but the tribe was desperate. And now desperation was about to pay off. The poor men would not have died in vain.

They would have healthy breeding stock again to replenish their numbers and the fortress-dwellers would not. The tables would turn, and soon, the tribe would hold the fortress and cast out the Williams to live in the hills and tunnels and wild places that only the brave dared explore.

He'd done his time exploring, bringing back anything of value he could find. Food was scarce, but here and there, stashes still could be discovered in long ago forgotten root cellars and storm shelters. Sometimes those places yielded food and sometimes only served as bait piles for live game. Rats, in particular, were good for ruining hidden stores, but offered up a significant food source of their own.

Phillip guessed the fortress-dwellers had never eaten rats. They had real livestock, after all.

From the inside, the fortress walls seemed

smaller, less ominous, just piles of broken concrete, remnants of the buildings that had once stood nearby. Here, there were no hints of the rusty barbed wire and metal spikes that were embedded in the outside. The wooden layer at the top looked tired and showed signs of rot and neglect. He noted the sun and his position and then the weaker spots on the wall and the way the walkway was built. When he returned home, he'd have a wealth of information to share.

Joshua snuck around the half-open booth where an empty chair sat. "No new William."

"Good. Open the door."

Joshua nodded, pulling the keys from his pocket. He set Phillip in the chair and stretched his back. With a sigh, he started going through the keys, one by one, trying them in the door to the vault.

"Does it only take one?"

"There are lots of holes."

Phillip groaned. "How about you bring that chair over there, and I'll give them a try?"

"If you want to." Joshua shrugged. He handed the keys to Phillip and then pushed the chair over to the door.

Only the top lock was out of reach, the rest he tried, one key in each until he'd found no success with it and then moved on. The first lock clicked. He flipped to the next key.

Someone called out, "What are you doing there?"

Phillip froze, hunched over the locks. Joshua

stood stick straight beside him.

"Nothing," said Joshua.

"Well then, go do something. There's work in the garden to be done. We don't feed you so that you can stand about. Unless you're helping William?"

Phillip peeked around Joshua, just enough to see the silhouette of a Jack walking away. "He'll be on garden duty as soon as we're finished here," he said in his best impersonation of a William's high-pitched voice.

The Jack nodded and wandered off.

Joshua sagged against him. Phillip calmed his racing pulse. He pulled the next key out of the row and was rewarded with a click.

Phillip wiped his brow and worked on the last of the two locks he could reach. "Let me know if you see that Jack again."

"Okay. You aren't really going to make me go work in the garden, are you? I'm very tired."

"No. I just said that to make the Jack go away."

"You lied. Lying is bad."

"Do you want to go work in the garden?"

Joshua shook his head.

"Then lying isn't so bad, is it?"

"Lying gets us in trouble."

"Telling the truth would have got us both killed. We're just lucky that one didn't get a good look at me. I'm a poor excuse for a William, that's for sure."

"You're nicer than a William." Joshua patted Phillip's shoulder.

"Thanks, Joshua." He needed to remember to

remain nice, or he'd find himself stranded in the fortress.

He got the third and fourth lock opened. "Now then, you're going to have to start at the beginning, but one of these must open that top lock. Can you try it?"

Joshua took the key ring and started going through them all. Phillip took his turn on lookout duty. Though, now if they were caught, it would be obvious that something was amiss.

A key slipped in and turned.

"Thank god!" Phillip would have leapt out of the chair if his feet would have held him. "Pick me up."

Joshua lowered himself so that Phillip could get his arms back around the boy's shoulders. Even for a Simple, he was more muscular than most of the men in his tribe. The poor men of his tribe tended to be frail of both body and mind, prone to sickness, and even if not used to lure the bullets of the Jacks on the walls, rarely lived to their twenties.

Joshua appeared healthy and strong. His clothes, though ill-fitting and patched were whole and smelled far better than his own. They must have plenty of supplies here. Maybe Joshua could manage to steal some on their way out, something to make the coming winter more comfortable for his tribe.

"How far until the women?"

Joshua groaned. "A long way."

As they headed away from the sunlight, Phillip marveled at the clean floors and working lights overhead. When they did find electricity, it was chancy at best and deadly at worst. Here, he could have believed the tales of generations past were only months old. No decay, rats, mold, cracks or litter marked the passing of years. Only the lanky man beneath him with his limited mind and flatish face confirmed that mankind wasn't on the same path it had once been.

He considered telling the boy to set him aside in the hall so that Joshua could make better time. The faster they freed the women, the sooner they could escape. They had the key ring. With it, they could open the outer doors and hopefully evade the watchful eyes of the Jacks. The Jacks wouldn't fire if they had women with them.

But if Joshua left him behind, would the boy come back for him? Would he hide in the vault somewhere, leaving Phillip to be discovered by the next William to wander in when he found the unlocked door?

"I'm sorry, Joshua. Can you manage to carry me with you?"

"I'll try."

"Thank you."

Phillip clung to Joshua's shoulders, trying not to pay attention to the pain in his feet each time he jostled against the boy. They walked down the long sloping hall until they reached a corner where the sunlight disappeared and only the artificial light was left to shine on them.

Around the first corner, he spotted a single doorway. No lights shown through the slotted window at the top of the door. The next corner yielded a similar view as did the third. "How far down does this go?"

"Too far." Joshua panted. "I need to rest."

"We don't have time to rest, Joshua." He tried to keep the irritation out of his voice.

"Then I will fall over and die like William."

He could feel the boy shaking beneath him. "Okay, maybe just a little while." The thought of sitting on the cold floor again didn't thrill him. "Is there somewhere out of the hallway we can hide while we rest?"

"Yes." Joshua set off with a more determined gait. Moments later, they arrived at an open door. "Arianne's room," he announced.

"The girl you killed?"

"She hurt me."

"Did she now? That wasn't nice of her." He sighed as Joshua set him down on the bed. A soft bed. And sheets. Bloody, but he didn't really care. How long had it been since he'd had sheets? These even smelled like sunshine and fresh breezes. "This is heavenly." He stretched out his arms and his back, rolling his head side to side on the thick pillows. "Why wasn't I born a woman?"

Joshua's forehead wrinkled. "You'd be an ugly woman."

Phillip stared at the boy for a moment and then burst out laughing. "You have a good point. The Williams would have cast me out the moment they caught sight of this face on a woman's body."

Joshua cracked a smile. "You can rest here. I'll be back soon."

Caution tugged at Phillips mind. "Joshua, how did Arianne hurt you?"

"A knife. The mothers have them. That's how they stabbed Jack."

"All the women have them?"

"I think so."

"Where did she hurt you?"

He held up his arms, showing the gashes on the backsides of his forearms. Dried blood colored his sleeves.

"Why didn't you say something? You should go get those cleaned out and put something on them. Do you have bandages here?"

Joshua nodded. "I didn't use them all on Jack."

"And water?"

"In the bathroom."

"A working bathroom?"

The boy nodded. "Clean and pretty."

"Damn." He wished he could get up and go see it for himself, but the bed was so comfortable that he could almost forget about the thumping pain in his feet.

No wonder the women here bore such healthy children. They wanted for nothing! Food, clothing, soft beds, pillows, even a bathroom with running water. Phillip shook his head. Arming them had to be an idea born by the Williams. That they didn't use their knives on the Jacks sent to mate with them hinted at some form of negotiation. Perhaps that was why they had so many luxuries.

Phillip felt his eyes slip closed but was too tired to open them. He'd just take a short nap. Maybe if he got some rest he'd be in a better mindset to deal with Joshua and the armed women.

CHAPTER EIGHT

Joshua marveled at his bandaged arms. Williams didn't often share the medical supplies with Simples. They certainly wouldn't if they knew what he'd done. He found Phillip sound asleep and decided it would be easier for his back to go talk to the mothers without him.

He crept down the hall, keeping away from the doors. His back ached and his legs ached. His empty stomach rumbled and his shoulders still felt heavy as if Phillip were hanging from them, but he trudged onward.

A dark trail of Jack's blood on the otherwise clean, gray floor greeted him at the bottom. Jack was dead.

His insides quaked like the floorboards of an old building about to collapse. If he could get the mothers to come with him, Phillip would be happy and take him away. But the voice inside didn't want them to come. They'd killed Jack.

Some of them did, he reminded himself. Most of them had no part in it. He remembered their faces, scared like his friends had been when the Wildmen set the buildings on fire.

The lock hung from the chain again. They couldn't hurt him unless he let them out. He took a deep breath and walked up to the barred doors.

Grandma rushed over to him, a scowl on her face. "What are you doing here again? What is going on with those Williams? Get back up top where you belong."

He refused to look at her, instead focusing on the nurse mothers. "You belong up top too. I have keys. I can bring you there."

The nurse mothers watched him. Some of the other mothers did too. None of them moved to form a big huddle like they did when Jack was there.

Grandma inserted herself between him and the mothers so he couldn't help but see her. "Where on earth did you get keys? We can't have this kind of negligence."

"From William-fourteen."

"He gave them to you? Is there something wrong up there?"

"William-fourteen got sick and died. Jack-three is dead too. And the William by the door. And Arianne."

The mothers began to all talk at once. Grandma waved at them to be quiet. Most of them kept talking and some crept toward the doors, which made Grandma's scowl even deeper.

"What's going on, Simple? Tell me," ordered Grandma.

"They take your babies and bury them in the

garden. They don't fix them. They kill them."

The nurse mothers wailed. One of the pretty mothers grabbed Grandma's arm. "Did you know this?"

She spun around to face the mother. "Of course I knew. They don't keep secrets from me. What did you think happened to them?" She shook her head. "Use your brain, girl. We can't afford more mouths to feed, certainly not ones that can't offer anything in return."

"Those boys were no different than us," said a nurse mother with a dark-skinned boy on her hip. "You think we offer nothing?"

"They can't have babies, so yes, they're different," said Grandma. "Now, go sit down and take care of your children, Grace."

"I want to go with Joshua."

"Don't be stupid. No one is leaving."

Sick of listening to Grandma, Joshua took the keys from his pocket and inserted them one by one into the lock.

Muriel joined Grandma. "We can't go out there. The germs will kill us. Remember the history the Matron has taught us."

"And where will you go?" said Grandma. "The Williams and Jacks will not allow you to endanger yourselves up there. You'll be sent right back down, and we'll all be punished for your idiotic actions."

The lock clicked open. Joshua removed it from the chain and threw it across the room behind him. It clattered across the cement floor. The women went silent.

"Phillip will give you a new place to live. He won't kill your babies. You will be free with the Wildmen."

"Who's Phillip?" asked the pretty mother wearing a green dress.

"The man Jack shot, that got put in jail. Then William-fourteen died before he could kill me, and Phillip said he could help me. He said he could help you too. I want to be free. Don't you?"

"Emelda, you get away from him."

"Matron, I'm leaving, and I'm sure I'm not the only one." Emelda glanced at the other mothers. Some of them nodded.

Grandma's jaw got so tight that he could see the muscles underneath her skin quiver like a scared puppy. "I've had enough of this. Everyone that doesn't have a knife, against the back wall. The rest of you, take care of this Simple."

Joshua's hands froze on the doors he was just about to open wide. Grace, Emelda, and several others rushed to the doors with children in their arms.

"No one will hurt you, Joshua," said another of the pretty mothers who stood beside Emelda. "Open the doors."

He hoped she was right. He didn't want to get hurt again. Joshua opened the doors.

Grandma came forward with a knife in her bony hand. "I have lived seventy-six long years because I have stayed safe inside. I bore healthy daughters and sons. I will not have my daughters out there if it means they will only bear the likes of you or worse."

Muriel had a knife in her hand too. Other mothers were busy grabbing children, some running to the back wall, some rushing out the door.

Two other mothers joined Grandma and Muriel.

They didn't deserve the nice things that he and his friends worked so hard to bring back to the fortress. His friends died protecting these women. Jack died just trying to bring Muriel a present. He wanted to hurt them, but if he did, the other girls would be afraid of him. He had to show them that Simples were nice, that he would never bite or hit them. He clenched his fists and then let them relax. Breathing deep, he let the smooth, low voice rise up inside him, filling him, making him strong.

"You four can't come with. Anyone else who wants to leave can leave with me. We'll have food and a place to live and be free. No one will tell us what to do. We'll all be like the Williams."

Women and children crowded around him, keeping Grandma and the others away.

"Get this silly dream out of your head and get back in here. We have more important things to do than listen to the idle chatter of a Simple."

He glared at the old woman. "I'm not a Simple. Not anymore."

"It's not something you get over," she said in an angry voice that said she would be hitting him on the ears if there wasn't a row of bodies between them. "It's how you were born."

She turned to the women still inside the room, looking at each one until she had their attention. "What I've told you is true. There are no cleaner places, no safer places, than this one. Isaiah looked."

"We're like him," said Grace, pointing at Joshua. "We can go outside."

"Shut up. I wasn't talking about you." Grandma focused on Emelda and the other pretty girls around Joshua. "It used to be that we were the many, and he was the few. If you leave, you're giving up any hope that we will return to how it should be. You'll be throwing away generations of careful breeding."

Now that the women were more spread out, Joshua glanced at them all, searching. "Which one of you is my mother? I want her to come too."

"You stupid boy," Grandma yelled. "No one knows who your mother is. Simples are taken from their mothers as soon as they show the signs. They're given to the nurses. The rest of us can't be bothered to care for the likes of you. We need to pay attention to the Isaiahs, Williams, and Jacks. Those are the important ones. Not you."

Tears gathered in his eyes, but he blinked them away. "You were all very bad. You killed an important Jack. He was my friend and he protected us all. A William will punish you, probably hit you, make you go without food for days, and take away your clothes."

The other two mothers put their knives down and backed away from Grandma and Muriel. Grandma's voice shook. "Don't listen to him. The

Williams would never hurt us."

She looked over everyone who stood on the other side of the doors. "Fine, leave then, but you can't take the good children."

Joshua grinned. "They can take anyone they want. Everyone will be important in our new home."

His stomach rumbled, reminding him how empty it was. "All of you with no babies to carry, go back and carry food. Then we won't be hungry while we walk to our new home."

"Oh no, no. You will not take our food or our good children. If you nurses want to leave, go on and take your Simples with you, but all the Jacks, Williams and Isaiahs must stay behind."

"No," said one of the nurse mothers. Her shoulders were very crooked, making one arm look longer than the other, but her eyes looked like the other pretty mothers and she spoke as clearly as they did. She clutched the hand of the young boy beside her. "They come with us. You have your own babies. These ones are ours."

"They are not yours. You help with them. That's all. These children belong to all of us. They are our future."

Grace stood beside her, the one boy on her hip and another older one holding the stump just below her elbow where her arm ended, both the deep brown color of Jacks who spent long years under the sun, guarding the walls. "These babies came from my belly. They are mine."

"The Isaiah's were implanted, you idiot. You

gave birth to them but they don't belong to you."

"My body might not be as whole as yours, but I'm not an idiot. I care for these boys. I gave birth to them." She pointed to the pretty girl beside Emelda. "You cared for Madeline. You say you gave birth to her. Does that mean she belongs to you?"

Grandma's lips got all scrunched up. "She's my daughter."

The nurse mother put a hand on both boys. "These are my sons, and we're leaving."

Madeline nodded. "We deserve a future too."

"Your future is here," said Grandma.

"You call sitting in a room alone until we're pregnant and then sitting here with a baby until they come take it away from us a future? I don't."

Joshua looked at the crowd gathered around him and warmth spread through his belly. More mothers stood outside the room than were left inside it. He won. Grandma lost. And in that moment, he closed his eyes and looked at the man who talked with the low smooth voice and decided that he wasn't scared of that man anymore. He was that man. He might be hollow and unfinished, but he could be worked with and polished, and one day, he would look at himself and see the face of the voiceman and they would smile the same smile and he would be whole and finished. Complete.

He wasn't a Jack or a William or even an Isaiah, he was a Joshua and that was just fine.

He closed the door and started up the ramp with the women and children following behind.

"You get back here!" said Grandma.

"I'm going with my friends, mother." Madeline held the hands of the two children beside her, one boy and one girl. "I will not sit here one more day and listen to half-remembered stories of how things once were. I want to go see how things are now. For myself, not from the guesses we put together from the men who visit our beds. I want to see the sun and smell the fresh breezes, to see the gardens and the dogs."

"You'll die. All of you." Grandma's voice cracked. "Please, leave the children. They don't deserve the fate you're bringing upon yourselves."

Madeline turned around. "Then sit here, Matron," she nearly spat the word, "safe and secure in the knowledge that you were right and we are all wrong."

"No!" Grandma ran to the doors. "Madeline, don't go. For God's sake, leave the children here. We need them!"

Madeline pulled her little boy closer. "Maybe we need them too." She turned to Joshua. "Take us to this Phillip."

He nodded and grinned from ear to ear as he marched along at the head of a crowd of mothers and children. The hall was no longer quiet with only the echoes of his footsteps to keep him company. This time, the mothers whispered to one another and children chattered and babies cried. Phillip would be very happy.

CHAPTER NINE

Joshua was so intent on getting everyone out of the vault that if he hadn't heard Phillip's snoring, he would have walked right past Arianne's room.

He wanted to talk to Phillip alone to make sure he wasn't mad about all the children. Getting yelled at in front of all the mothers would make them laugh at him, and he didn't think he could bear that.

Joshua held up his hand and went to the door. "Wait here. I'll be right back."

"Wake up!" he yelled in Phillip's face. "The mothers are here and we want to leave."

The little man sat up and wiped his eyes. "How many did you get?"

"Lots and children too."

Phillip scowled. "Children? That will make things more difficult. Can we leave them behind?"

The mothers wouldn't like that. "There are Isaiahs, Williams, and Jacks. Don't you want them too?"

Phillip's jaw fell open. "You have child Isaiahs? We thought they were all gone. Our scouts haven't spotted an Isaiah in years." He grinned. "By all means, we'll take the children too." He held up his arms. "Pick me up."

Joshua sat on the edge of the bed. Sitting felt good. Lying down would feel better. The bed was so soft under him. He yawned.

Phillip's arms snaked around his shoulders. "Come on, no time for dawdling. We've got to get these women out of here."

Joshua sighed and got to his feet with the little man firmly attached to his back.

"Have each woman take something from this room. We'll need all the supplies we can carry if we are to bring so many with us."

Joshua halted. "But you said you had food."

"I do," Phillip said quickly. "But it would make things easier on these women if they have some of the comforts they are used to."

"Oh, okay." These mothers were used to having everything done for them. And it made some of them mean. Maybe once they'd lived under the blue sky, they would be nice again. He could fix them. Joshua smiled to himself.

He went out the door with Phillip on his back. "Everyone go inside and take one thing with you."

"Or more, if you can carry it," Phillip added.

"So you will be happy on our trip." Joshua waved the girls toward the door.

One of the nurses left her children in the care of one of the Simples and wandered inside. She screamed.

She must have spotted Arianne. Dread flooded through Joshua. Would the girls think he was bad now? Would they turn him over to the Williams? He rushed to the doorway to keep any of the others from going inside.

Phillip tugged his arms. "What is she screaming about?"

"Arianne. She's dead."

"You left me in a room with a dead woman?"

Joshua shrugged. "She was dead. She couldn't hurt you. Not like she did me."

"What's wrong in there? Are you hurt?" asked Madeline. She tried to push her way past Joshua.

"I'll check on her," he said. "Keep everyone out here so they're out of the way."

Joshua went in with Phillip on his back and pulled the door closed behind him. No one followed, but he could hear their murmurs right outside.

Phillip whispered, "You killed her?"

"I hit her after she cut me, and then she fell and hit her head."

"Well that won't make you very popular with the ladies, now will it?"

The voiceman inside Joshua began to waver, leaving him uncertain and afraid. If the women wouldn't follow him out of the fortress, he'd have to go with Phillip alone, and Phillip would be angry. It would be worse than being with angry Williams. At least he knew what angry Williams would do to him. He had to make this all better.

Joshua walked over to the nurse mother who stood, rocking back and forth, arms folded across her chest. "It's okay. She's in a better place now." That's what Williams always told them when someone died. It felt odd to be the one saying those words, but it wasn't a bad kind of odd. Instead, it made him feel strong inside again.

He placed his hand gently on her shoulder and turned her away from Arianne. "We need to choose our supplies before a William comes."

The nurse mother nodded, gathered up an armload of blankets and hurried out of the room.

Phillip sighed, his sour breath wafting across Joshua's face. "Tell them Jack did it."

"I can't do that. That would be a lie."

"So?"

"Lying is bad. It gets us in trouble."

"I see. Let me take care of this then. Open the door."

Joshua's hand shook as he pulled the door open. He really didn't want the girls mad at him, but he didn't want Phillip mad at him either.

Phillip ducked around Joshua's head. "Excuse me, if I could have your attention. It seems that the Jack who was here earlier killed this woman."

It worried Joshua that Phillip lied to the girls. If Phillip lied to them now, what else would he lie about? Yet, he was relieved that the girls would not be scared of him.

"Perhaps Joshua would be so kind as to cover up the poor girl so that none of the rest of you need to look at her," said Phillip.

"Okay." Joshua went back inside, carrying Phillip along with him. He pulled the sheet from the bed and covered Arianne with the half that Jack hadn't bled on.

The mothers milled in the hallway, talking amongst themselves. What he could make out sounded like mad words about Jack. It made him sad. Jack hadn't done anything wrong. Not really.

The mothers came in one by one, grabbing something to take with before ducking back out into the hall.

Emelda knelt down next to Arianne, pulling back the sheet to see her face. "I can't believe she's dead. Death from childbirth or sickness is one thing, but this?" She shook her head.

At a loss for what to say, he repeated one of the things Williams often told Simples who were upset. "It will be okay."

She looked up at him. "How do you know that? We're leaving our home, the only home we've ever known and all because this man that can't even walk says he has somewhere else for us to live."

"Don't worry," Phillip said. "My people will take good care of you. And you'll be free, not kept in cages."

Emelda replaced the sheet over Arianne. "We've been told you are the ones the Jacks and Williams are protecting us from."

"They're selfish and want to keep you for themselves. They don't even let you outside, do they?"

She shook her blonde curls.

"That's not very nice of them at all. We will let

you outside as much as you want."

"That would be nice."

"And you can pick your own mates. No one will do it for you."

Her eyes lit up and she smiled a tiny smile.

"Now go pick something to bring with you. Clothes, supplies, anything. Are there other rooms that we can get supplies from?"

"The Matron says there aren't as many of us as there once were. The rooms we use for breeding are all well stocked. "

"We'll look on our way out then. Thank you."

All this running around and then waiting made Joshua nervous. "The Williams will find the open door soon. We should go."

"We will. We need these supplies, Joshua. Besides, if a William or a Jack wanders down here, they will be confronted with a horde of women armed with knives. They weren't afraid to kill a man before, why would this be any different? If anything, they will be more willing now that they know whoever stands in their way, stands in the way of their freedom."

That made sense, but he still felt all jittery inside.

The women went in and out, working like bees gathering pollen for their hive. They swarmed in the hall with food and supplies in boxes and packed into rolled clothes, blankets and towels.

As they waited, Joshua had a hard time standing still. Sweat gathered on his hands and trickled down the sides of his face. He licked his lips and counted the women. Fourteen of them, mostly nurses, a few Simples and the three pretty mothers. The children kept moving, making them hard to count. He tried twice and then gave up, trusting that the girls knew how many they had with them.

"So where are we going?" One of the Simples asked.

Joshua glanced over his shoulder at Phillip.

"We have keys. We'll be walking up to the door and down the path to the nearest patrol exit, where Joshua here will open the lock and let us out. Once on the outside, I will lead us to the hills where my tribe lives, and we'll get you settled in."

The mothers smiled, gathered up their children and belongings and parted to let Joshua and Phillip through. Relieved to finally be moving, Joshua hurried through the crowd and started up the ramped hall.

"Don't forget to stop at the empty rooms," Phillip said in his ear.

"Can't we just go"? asked Joshua. "If a William finds us—"

"We need supplies. We have keys. We'll hurry."

Joshua sighed and at the next door with no lights on, pulled out his key ring and started testing the keys. Certain keys now looked familiar. He quickly passed over those and tried the others. One turned in the new lock.

The door swung open. He reached inside and felt for a light switch. One bulb flickered to life, buzzing loudly.

Phillip said, "Take what you can and let's go ahead and find another room."

Girls gathered more things to carry. Even the older children carried something.

Joshua shuffled from foot to foot. He felt alive and excited but also scared. Very scared.

The high pitched voice of a William cut through the bustle of room raiding. "What is going on here?" His eyes grew wide as his gaze came to rest on Phillip's head bobbing next to Joshua's. "How did you get out? Simple, is this your doing?"

Joshua cringed. He never wanted to be called Simple again, but he'd been bad and he knew it. He wanted to set Phillip down and tell the women to go back to their room. He wanted to make William happy with him again.

Then the voice rose in his head and he remembered that the other William had said he would be killed and no one would miss him and that he wasn't really needed anyway. He thought of all the mean things Grandma had said. All the things he'd overheard his whole life swirled around his head.

He wasn't nobody. He was going to bring these girls out to see the blue sky and make them free and they would like him and no one would be mean to him ever again. And Phillip was going to help him. He grasped Phillip's arms and charged forward. "You go away. Leave us alone. We're done with you."

"Done?" William quirked an eyebrow. "What are you talking about? Calm down, Simple. What is your number?"

"I'm Joshua, and you're in my way." He pushed the big man aside and called back to the mothers. "We need to go. Come on."

William surged back at him. "Just where do you think you're going? You can't take these women outside. They'll die."

"No, they won't. Quit scaring them."

"I'm trying to protect them. The outside is dangerous. The children will get sick. The women will be attacked. We can't protect them outside. That's why they must stay in here."

Phillip said, "You keep these people like slaves. Brainwashed. If you want to stay safe in your vault, you go right ahead, fat man. The rest of us are going to be free."

The women whispered to one another. Joshua noticed that Emelda, Madeline, and the other pretty mother had knives, but the rest didn't. Did they use the knives to protect themselves against the Simples and nurses too? He shook his head. Knives had killed Jack. No more knives.

But even as he made the declaration to himself, the three pretty mothers ran ahead of the others with their knives in their hands and they plunged them into the William.

Several of the children cried. One of the Simples screamed. The rest stayed back, clutching their children and supplies.

William gasped and stumbled sideways, smashing his back against the wall. He reached down to his stomach and then looked at the blood on his hand as he slipped down the wall. "What have you done?"

"We're done with this life," said Madeline. "We want our own. Our children deserve their own. You'll not take them from us any longer."

"Take them from you? We let you keep the girls. The boys have work to do. They keep you safe."

"We've watched our little boys be led away to be told their names mean nothing and that their childhood is silliness to be forgotten. You put a gun in their hands, or a hoe, or a breeding book and they forget about the women who loved them more than anything else. Don't you think that crushes us? Don't you think it hurts us to watch our daughters grow up only to have their children ripped away too?

"You think the boys don't wonder who their mothers were? You can't make them forget. Joshua remembers his name. He remembers his mother's face. He gave us hope that there is a better way, that we can all live together. We don't need this heartache, and we don't need you."

Emelda spat on William and looked to Joshua. "Get us out of here."

He nodded. They trudged up the hall. Their whispers had died down and even the children were quiet, but their steps were determined and the three pretty mothers walked behind him with their knives in their hands. Other women held their small children and their packs, sharing the load between them all.

Joshua led them up the hall, not stopping at the

dark doors or even the two with lights on. They needed to move quickly before more Williams came.

The keys rested heavy in his pocket. He'd killed today, but he'd not meant to. His arms ached when he thought of Arianne's pretty face staring at the door, unmoving, frozen in an endless gaze. He wouldn't cry out loud, but inside he told the pretty girl he was sorry and he cried for her. He didn't want to cry for anyone else. Not today, not ever.

He thought of his stuffed dog. He'd never see it again if he left. One of his friends would find it and hold it tight at night. Maybe it would help one of his friends to find his own voice deep inside.

Joshua smiled as he caught sight of the daylight at the end of the hall. The door stood open just a sliver.

The mothers murmured and the children chattered happy little sounds. Joshua pushed the door open and let the sunlight wash over him. He looked around but saw no one. Phillip let out a little whoop and pounded on Joshua's chest. They ventured out into the afternoon light and gave the women space to exit the vault.

"Quiet here," Joshua said. "The Jacks and Williams will hear you."

Exclamations of joy and wonder filled the air. Children gasped and clung to their mothers, their tiny mouths gaping as they looked around them.

"No. No! Be quiet." He paced about, shaking his head. Why did they have to be so loud? Why wouldn't they listen? Williams wanted to kill him.

They wanted to kill Phillip too.

As more of the women filtered out of the vault with shaded and squinting eyes, the jitters inside Joshua grew. It was one thing to get into trouble himself, but he didn't want these little children to suffer the wrath of the Williams.

The pretty mothers seemed able to take care of themselves, but the others were unarmed. They needed to be protected. And that fell to him and Phillip. And Phillip couldn't walk.

Joshua stood tall and puffed out his chest like Jacks did. He looked around, shielding his eyes from the sunlight to see the tops of the walls. The Jack on the wall had his back to them. Joshua glanced left and right but saw no one.

"Let's go, and please, stay quiet." He waved the Simple girls to follow him. They walked along in a long silent line, only the shuffling of feet on the pebbles of the walk revealing their passage through the fortress. And then a baby wailed.

Joshua spun around, nearly flinging Phillip off his back. "Quiet. Quiet!"

A nurse put her hand over the baby's mouth, but it did little to muffle the sound.

The Jack on the wall called out, "What's going on over there?" He held his hand above his eyes as he peered down.

Joshua could think of nothing to say that would give the mothers time to hide. If they'd even know where to hide. They'd never been up top before, he reminded himself. They didn't know how the Jacks and the Williams could be when they weren't being nice. His heart pounded. He kept walking. The women followed, clumping up behind him like a flock of chicks following a hen.

"Answer me, Simple. What's going on? Are those our women and children?"

Joshua walked faster, leading his followers between as many buildings as he could to keep them out of the Jack's view. He wanted to run, but he knew the children couldn't keep up and the mothers had their hands full of supplies and babies.

Overhead, the Jack called to another. In minutes all the Jacks on the walls would know how bad he was. And they had guns.

The patrol door lay straight ahead. If they could get there before anyone else saw them, he'd have time to find the key and get them outside.

"Don't worry," Phillip said. "They won't shoot at us if we stay with the women and children. We can do this, Joshua. Just keep walking. He won't be able to see us once we get next to the wall. Get your keys out now."

Joshua pulled the key ring from his pocket. He wanted to run ahead and get the door open, but if he left the mothers behind, the Jack might shoot him. Instead, he walked and traced each key with his finger, feeling for the unfamiliar ones to try in this new lock.

"Where are you going? Stop! Answer me, Simple," yelled the Jack on the wall.

Joshua hurried to the metal door with chipped

black paint at the end of the pebbled walk. Usually, a William sat there when his shift started. The William would unlock the door and send him out to do his run. Another would let him back in at the window door. He always knew he was safe when he saw the window with the William face in it. After the William let him in, he'd go report to Jack-three and then Jack-three would usually half-smile and nod and then tell him to go walk the paths again. But Jack-three wouldn't do that anymore.

Joshua's feet seemed to move slower. He knew the paths outside the door, but he didn't know what lay beyond them other than bears. Bears that ate his friends. He'd come across what was left of one of them. He remembered throwing up after finding him and the more he thought about it, the more his insides quivered. There would be no Jacks on this run telling him what to watch for or where to go, keeping him safe.

Jack shouted for a William, "There are women and children out in the open."

He took a deep breath. Jack-three was gone. Williams didn't like him anymore and he'd be in big trouble if they caught him. Phillip needed help getting outside the fortress walls and so did the mothers, but what did he want? He didn't know.

Strange things waited for him outside the walls. More Wildmen. Phillip seemed nice enough, but he also lied. Did that mean all the Wildmen lied? Would Phillip hurt him when he didn't need him to carry him anymore? He didn't know. He was sad to discover that he didn't know much at all. Without the Williams to tell him what to do, he was lost.

He'd snuck around a little at night, tiptoeing into the garden for a snack, but he knew the garden. He knew the pathways. He knew the buildings. He knew where his bunk was.

Joshua suddenly didn't want to leave. He'd open the door and let the women out. He'd put Phillip outside the wall. Then he'd lock the door again and go to sleep on his bunk and when he woke up everything would be right again.

The Jack shouted at the other one again, "Get someone on the ground to sort this out. We can't leave our posts."

"Joshua." Phillip boxed him in the ear. "Let's get that door open."

"I have to find key." He stared at the black door before him.

"Then find the key."

The mothers and the children gathered around him. Joshua pulled the first key from the ring. He began to try them in the lock.

The Jack yelled again, "There are women loose. And children. Over here."

Simples working in the melon field nearby looked up from their harvesting. One waved at Joshua. The others looked at the women and children and smiled. They all started toward the door.

"No, stay back," said Joshua. "Keep working." He had enough people to watch over and no time to explain to others the risks or how to help. For a moment, he felt like a William, giving orders.

"Hurry," Phillip yelled in his ear.

Joshua cringed. He flipped through the keys faster and faster, his hands shaking. "I'm trying."

A William barreled at him with a Jack right behind. The William said, "One-fifty-two, is it?"

Joshua froze and turned at the sound of the friendly voice.

"Don't listen to him," said Phillip.

"I—" It was William-four. He wanted to run to him, to explain, to beg for forgiveness.

"Open the door and you'll never have to answer his questions again. Just open the door, Joshua."

He nodded and tried the keys again.

"One-fifty-two, stop this nonsense. Come away from the door. Put that filthy man down. He has filled your head with lies."

"I haven't, Joshua. You know that. We can be free outside the door. Open it."

Joshua tried another key, but his hands shook so much he nearly dropped the ring. He caught them before they hit the ground. Phillip's weight careened to one side. The little man scrabbled at Joshua, tearing the shoulder of Joshua's shirt as he tumbled to the ground with an agonizing cry.

"That's right. Walk away from the Wildman," said William-four. "Women, head back to the vault. This Wildman cannot harm you and neither will One-fifty-two. Take your children and go back to your room."

Joshua turned to see the three pretty mothers on

the outside of their group, facing the William and the Jack with bloody knives in their hands.

"Breeders, are you hurt?" asked William-four.

"It's not our blood," said Madeline.

"What have you done?" William turned and called out, "William-eleven, check the vault. Now." When he again faced them, all trace of friendly was gone. He looked just like William-fourteen when he'd told Joshua he was going to be killed.

Joshua swallowed hard. The women bunched around him and Phillip, like they'd done down in the vault when they the children had hid behind them. Now he was with the children, safe behind the protective wall of mothers and nurses.

William waved his hand at them. "Jack-six, do something. Get One-fifty-two and the Wildman and put them in jail. Shoot them if they give you any trouble."

"They are surrounded by women and children. Would you chance harming them?"

"They must be stopped!"

"I'm not hurting the women and children."

"They're armed. They've obviously hurt someone. They'll need to be punished. Just don't shoot anything important."

"Are you mad? *They* are important. They are the whole reason we're here, walking the walls every day, killing men like him," he pointed into the crowd of women toward the ground where Phillip lay. "You think we enjoy killing anyone? We don't."

"Oh, shut up. Killing and breeding are about the

only things you Jacks are good for. Just do your job."

Joshua left them to their arguing and returned to his keys. William and Jack's voices got louder as he tried another and then another, but he didn't catch their words. The keys were more important.

Another Jack called down from the wall. "I can't get a clear shot from here."

"Then don't shoot," said Jack-six.

"Do something," William shrieked.

Phillip tugged at Joshua's pants. "Hurry."

The lock clicked.

The deafening sound of a rifle filled the air above them. The mothers screamed and the children cried. They crushed Joshua in their rush to get into the shadow of the doorway, rubbing against him and pinning all but his hands against the door.

"Hurry, Joshua," one of them breathed into his ear. The crush became ever so much worse, and his hands started to sweat. He turned the handle. It wouldn't open. He looked up and down the door. Another lock.

Joshua groaned and went to work on it.

Rifle fire again filled the air. Dirt spattered around them, dust choking them all.

"I said, fire a warning shot. What the hell are you doing?" Jack-six yelled.

"I aimed at the ground, not them."

"Put the damn rifle down before you hurt someone," said Jack-six.

"Don't you dare," said William-four. "Take out one of the Simple women. We have plenty more."

"Madeline, Susan, to the front. Everyone else, behind us," said Emelda. The women shifted around Joshua, pressing against the door so he barely had room to work on the lock.

"You're going to shoot one of us, William?" asked Madeline.

"Where do you think you're going?" asked Jack-six. "There's nothing out there. If you're unhappy, I'm sure you can talk with the Williams and find a solution."

"The solution is no more Williams," said Madeline. "You want a solution, well, there you have it."

Jack sounded closer. "Come on, it can't be all that bad. Did a William do something to you?"

"Yes, he tried to stop us from leaving."

The huddle jostled back and forth. Jack-six yelped.

"They cut me," he said, surprised.

"Then cut one back," said William.

"I wasn't even on duty. I don't have any weapons on me."

"Some Jack you are."

The last lock clicked. The handle turned. Joshua bumped the women backward and pulled the door open. "Go!"

They poured through the door as if a drain plug had been pulled. He gathered Phillip into his arms and ran outside as the crowd flowed around them. Children spilled out, tumbling to the ground and scrambling to their feet. Joshua shoved the keys into his pocket, held on tight to Phillip, and ran.

Jack-six ran after them with the William close behind. "Come back! Where are you going! It's not safe out there!"

Madeline threw a handful of dirt and rocks in Jack's face before picking up one of the lagging children and catching up with the others.

Jack coughed but stayed close behind.

Phillip leaned close to Joshua's ear. "Don't listen to them. Just run. Run as fast as the women can. Stay together and head north. We'll reach my people in a couple days."

"We can't run for days."

"We can walk as soon as we leave the fortress behind."

"We have to walk at night?" Night was when the bears were really bad. Night was dark, and he didn't know where he was out here. No baying of the dogs to let him know he was near the kennel, no cross-shaped moon shadows to tell him he was near the garden. No familiar creaks of the walks as the Jacks patrolled the walls. The ground was uneven here, no pebbled or cracked paths under his feet.

Trees, plants—everything looked different from what he remembered from his runs along the patrol path. He glanced over his shoulder. The fortress was growing smaller. But some of the women were slowing already. They didn't have strong legs like he did. They didn't run patrols around the entire fortress several times a night. They didn't work in the gardens or build walls. They were weak. And he was strong.

He was like a Jack. Joshua smiled to himself and ran on with Phillip clinging to him.

"Get back here! You don't know what you're doing!" William yelled.

Joshua could hear Jack's heavy footsteps pounding after them.

The Jack on the wall fired again. The sound of the rifle echoed in his head. They wouldn't fire at him, not with the mothers so close. Phillip was right. He hadn't lied about that.

Children screamed. Joshua turned to see Jack grabbing hold of two dark-haired little boys, the back of his hand dripping blood on the shirt of the boy in his right hand. The boys kicked and screamed but remained helpless in the big hands of the Jack. The crowd halted. Their arms still full of supplies and babies, there was little the women could do but wail in protest. The three pretty mothers stalked Jack like a big cat hunting a mouse.

"Stop," Joshua said. He set Phillip down and walked toward Jack-six. "Let them go."

"No. You have no idea what you're doing, Simple."

"Maybe I do."

Red-faced, William-four caught up to them, huffing and puffing. "You're going to ruin everything! You're endangering the hope of humanity!"

"You're the one endangering everything," Phillip said.

"Enough." William signaled to the Jack on the

wall. The rifle burst through the air again. One of the Simple girls screamed. Blood seeped through the sleeve of her yellow dress.

Children cried, their tears trailing over dusty cheeks. Grace handed her child to another and wrapped her arm around the hurt girl.

William said to the wounded girl, "Come here, dear, let me have a look at that. We'll get you fixed up good as new."

She held her arm, tears streaming down her cheeks as she wailed, "He hurt me!"

"Come now, let me have a look at that. We'll go back inside, and I'll make it all better." He spoke with the kind voice Joshua remembered, but now he'd seen the ugly face behind that voice. William-four was no different than the others.

Susan placed herself between the Simple and William. "You stay right there. We're not going anywhere with this William or any other. We've made our decision. A new life. No more cages."

The Simple clutched her arm. "But it's scary out here, and my arm hurts."

"You're only hurt because he," Madeline pointed at William, "told the Jack to fire his gun. It's his fault. If we leave him, there's no reason to be scared anymore."

Jack shook his head. "Is that so? Did the Simple or the Wildman tell you about the bears? I bet they didn't."

"Bears?"

"Yes, huge hairy, stinky animals with long claws

and sharp teeth. They'd love to eat you."

Madeline said, "Joshua will protect us from the bears."

Jack's dark brows rose, wrinkling his forehead right up to his bald scalp. "Really? A Simple? Do you have any idea how many Simples the bears eat every month?"

The pretty mothers stood together with their knives in their hands. "Then the Wildman will keep us safe."

William laughed. "The Wildman is half-dead."

"He knows where the safe places are. We'll be fine. He lives out here. He can keep us safe."

"Is that so?" William raised his hand.

The rifle fired.

Phillip cried out.

William stood on his tiptoes and peered around the women. He smiled. "I don't think the Wildman is going to help you anymore. Now, how about we forget this ever happened and we go back inside? Bring the children."

The pretty mothers looked at one another. Joshua fumed. How could William have Phillip shot like that? He looked down at the poor Wildman. He was coughing blood and holding his hand over the big hole in his stomach where blood was pouring out.

"Joshua," he said between coughs. "Get them to safety. Don't listen to the Williams or the Jacks. My people will welcome you. There is a coin in my pocket. Take it and walk away with the women and children. Keep to the middle of the crowd and the Jack won't dare fire at you. Go north."

He knelt down next to Phillip and felt around in his pocket. His fingers rubbed over a round metal disc the size of the end of his thumb. He held up a silver circle.

Phillip nodded. "Now leave me and go. North."

"Which way?"

His body shuddered. An arm flopped out, sending up a puff of dust as it landed. Bloody spittle gathered on his lips and then his chest stopped moving.

Joshua nodded. "This way," he said to the women. "Let's go."

"But he's got my boys," One of the nurses protested. "I won't leave without my boys."

William grabbed one of the boys from the Jack. "They weren't yours anyway. They belong to us."

The boy squirmed. "Let me go!"

"Quiet down now. We'll get you back home in no time. You shouldn't be out here. You'll get sick."

The mother looked to Joshua.

"He's lying. We'll be fine." Joshua made sure to keep himself in the middle of the crowd of mothers and children.

"I wouldn't lie, Simple. Lying is bad. We've taught you that."

Joshua squared his aching shoulders and glared at William. "I'm not lying when I say that we'll be fine outside the walls."

William scowled. It was then that Joshua knew

that William-four did lie. And if William lied about this, he had probably lied about other things. A deep sadness flooded through him.

"Joshua?" Emelda said, nodding to William.

He wished he didn't know what she was asking, but he did. The three pretty mothers were all covered with spatters of blood. It made them not so pretty anymore. In fact, they kind of scared him, but he needed them. They had knives and they weren't afraid to use them. He just hoped they didn't use them on him.

He nodded.

She leaned close to the other two and whispered something. They surged toward William and the boy. "Give him to us, William. We'll let you go."

He glanced at the knives but otherwise ignored them. Jack took a step closer. William shook his head. He spoke loud and even just like he did when giving orders to the Jacks and Simples. "Let me go? I say what goes around here. Forget this madness and get back in the vault. There will be no hot, healthy meals out here, believe me. You'll be dining on rats and mushrooms for the rest of your days."

Susan gulped but stood her ground. "Then we will learn to enjoy rats and mushrooms, but we will be free."

Sweat shimmered on his reddened brow and beaded on his upper lip. "Freedom? Is that what this Wildman has filled your little minds with a thirst for? Freedom brought us here, where we are safe. Free people came here and built these walls to keep the raiders out. The brightest minds of the free men and women came here so that they could work to better our way of life and make us whole again. You are descended from them. How are you anything but free?

"You're safe and cared for. If you go to the Wildmen, you will be their slaves."

Madeline waved her knife in William's face. William's gaze followed the blade, but Jack's were on the crowd.

"We're slaves here," she said. "We're leaving with Joshua and our children. My mother is in the vault with her sycophants, timid things that they are." She spat on the ground. "Go ask them to spread their legs for you."

Jack-six took one of his hands off the boy in his grasp to rest it heavily on William's shoulder. "Why are most of these women so malformed? Are there male Simples hidden in the vault that are like them?"

The boy in his wounded grasp twisted free and dashed to his nurse mother. He stood there, clutching her skirts and sobbing.

"Don't worry, Jack," said William, glancing between Jack's hand and Madeline's knife. "We can talk about it once we get these women back to the vault where they belong. They are the treasure of our fortress, and we must make sure they are safe."

"Is that so? Weren't you just trying to get me to hurt them a few minutes ago?"

"It was for their own good."

Susan stepped forward. "Joshua told us that the

Williams kill the misshapen boys, but you won't find them in the graveyard. They bury them in the garden so you won't know. We didn't want to believe it, but the Matron confirmed what he said. That's the sort of thing Williams do for our own good."

William's eyes got so big, Joshua worried that they'd fall out of his face. Jack pried Williams fingers from the boy the fat man still held. Once free, the boy ran to his mother.

"I've never seen a single William caring for a sick baby outside the vault, and I can't say that I recall seeing any fresh small graves," said Jack. "How is it that you take the babies from the women and they end up in the gardens, William?"

The fat man cleared his throat. "You don't need to worry about the babies. It's not your job."

Jack's jaw trembled and the veins on his forehead stood out like worms just under the surface. "You've been feeding us with food grown from our own children?"

"It's how they best serve our community. The soil needs fertilizer.

Jack turned to William, all but ignoring the mothers with knives.

"We knew you wouldn't understand," said William. "That's why we didn't inform you."

"I suppose you thought we wouldn't understand how the Simples keep harvesting the same amount of food as always but our rations keep getting cut. We figured that out pretty quick when Jack-three discovered a stockpile of food in William-five's house."

William sputtered.

"One-fifty-two here isn't the only one who can open a lock."

"That food is for the future. It's for when the Isaiahs find a cure. It's not for us. It's for the good of all of us."

"You're starving the Simples, the ones who do all the work around here, but clearly you're not starving yourselves." He shoved a finger into William's belly. "I saw the horde of food under his bed with my own eyes. Your version of what's good for our future isn't ours."

The knuckles on the hand Jack had on William's shoulder went white. William winced.

Jack said, "If the deformed women grow up, why wouldn't the boys? I think you're just too busy sitting around and sneaking extra meals in your houses to deal with them. Maybe if you Williams didn't eat so damn much, we'd have plenty of food for those children.

"Even the Wildmen found uses for their deformed. We could be sending them out on patrols so we don't lose the Simples, like this one, who can follow directions and do useful work. Each Simple we lose hurts our workforce."

A tiny ball of warmth built in Joshua's chest. Jack-six did think he was worth something. It was the Williams who were bad.

"We have plenty of Simples," said William as he tried to pull away.

The Jack on the wall watched them. Another Jack rounded the corner of the fortress walk and joined him. Both of them had their guns raised.

"Our boys could have had a purpose? You killed them for nothing?" asked Susan. "Were they even dead when you tossed their tiny bodies into the dirt?"

The mothers looked ready to set their children aside and rip the William apart with their bare hands. Joshua was very glad at that moment to be born a Joshua and not a William.

With his face only inches from the trembling fat man, Jack said, "Take your children and go. All of you. I'll deal with the Williams." He held up his hand to the Jacks on the walls.

Joshua didn't need to be told to go twice. He checked which way Phillip had pointed. The mothers gathered up their children and their packs and cast one last look at the Jack and the William who were now screaming at each other, and at the Jacks on the wall, watching them all with rifles in their hands.

Joshua paused by Phillip. His chest didn't go up and down anymore like it was supposed to. Joshua left his eyes open so that Phillip could see them all doing what he'd wanted. He waved at the Wildman. Joshua smiled as several of the nurse mothers and Simples stopped to wave too as they passed by. He headed into the low-lying tangle of weeds and bushes growing among toppled ruins of buildings with the women and children following close behind.

CHAPTER TEN

The more Jack-six thought about what he'd just learned, the more he began to question all the things the Williams had told him—things that were done because they'd been done since he was a child. Jacks left the big room at the bottom the vault when they were four. They were taken to a house to live with two Williams, where they were given chores, taught how to manage Simples and trained to fend off attacks from the Wildmen. As soon as they were proven dependable, they were sent off to live with the older Jacks. Most of his time with the pair of Williams was a blur of learning and excitement. Now he wished he'd been more daring, more willing to demand answers as the years had gone by.

William-four sputtered and fumed in his grasp. "They've taken two of the Isaiahs! Get them back!"

Jack watched the receding figures of the last of the women and children who had followed the Simple off into the wilds. Would they get the welcome they expected now that the captive was dead? If they even made it to the Wildmen. He half expected to find bedraggled children and their frantic mothers begging at the door by morning.

The day he'd been torn away from his mother, her eyes had been filled with tears as she watched him leave with his hand firmly held by a William. He'd never seen her again, but hazy memories of a big room filled with women and children tugged at his thoughts when he was alone out on the lonely walls.

"Why are you still standing here? Go. Run. Get those boys back." William knocked his weight into Jack, but it did nothing more than make him take a step sideways.

He couldn't remember seeing women like the misshapen ones he'd seen today, but his early memories were of smiling motherly faces, a few words to nonsense songs, and the few clear bits of his own mother.

"What the hell were you thinking, telling them to go? They didn't have permission to go," William yelled in Jack's face, spittle forming on his thick lips. "You're not trained to make decisions like this, Jack. That wasn't your place. You directly disobeyed orders."

Jack shoved the fat man away. The William stumbled backward.

As much as food cultivated muscle in Jacks, it produced fat in Williams. Then again, they did little but dispense orders and sit in chairs while supervising. Any walking was done at a leisurely waddle. He'd spend his childhood fixing buildings with heavy rocks and walking the walls. The Williams were weak.

William steadied his footing. "What do you think you're doing? You can't touch me!"

"Apparently I can." Jack glanced at his brother on the wall. The armed man watched them through his scope. He held his hand up and waved. The Jack on the wall relaxed his stance.

Did his mother give birth to any of the baby boys that fertilized the food they all ate? Would it have been more humane to toss the bodies over the wall for the bears? No, that would only make the bears stronger. At least this way, they were the ones benefitting from their own loses. There weren't many places within the fortress that lent themselves to gardening. It made a sort of sense that the Williams would need to continually fertilize the soil in order to keep it fertile. Yet, animal wastes were a palatable option than the dead.

"That Simple was right about one thing. You've lied to us all. I think it's about time one of you was punished. I can't remember ever seeing a William locked in the jail."

"Because we have the keys." William lifted his double chins and glared at him. "Without us, the fortress would fall apart. You Jacks may have the strength, but you don't know how to use your brains."

"Perhaps it's time we learn." Jack wrapped his hands around William's neck, holding him. "Besides, that's what we have the Isaiahs for."

William gasped. "They're children!"

"But they'll grow up. And without you, they'll

listen to us. They won't know it was ever any other way."

"There are more of us than there are of you," said William

"But with you gone, no one will warn the others of your extermination."

William gurgled something that sounded like, "Why?"

"Those are my brothers and my children you buried in the garden." Jack squeezed harder.

The fat man's face turned reddish-purple and his eyes bulged. He coughed and gagged and dug his fingernails into Jack's arms. His thick legs kicked and his body twisted, yet Jack held on.

William's head rolled forward and his body went limp. After another minute to make sure he was dead, Jack let go.

The Wildman lay on the ground, dead. The Simple and his followers were gone from sight. If they'd left Isaiahs in the vault, he had no need of the others. They could raise these Isaiahs to work with the Jacks rather than oversee them.

The Simple could wander off with the troublemakers and the deformed if it meant the reliable breeding base remained in the vault. Maybe he would find a mate he wouldn't have to share with the other Jacks.

He had his mind on a few Simples, the more able ones. He could promote them, give them ranks. The Jacks could move into the William's houses and give the higher Simples their base to help set them apart. If they ran their own kind, perhaps that would help alleviate any resentment. He could even reward those Simples with women too. There had to be some Simple women left. If Simples bred with Simples, they wouldn't object, would they? And the other women wouldn't have to be with one unless they wanted to. Maybe some of them would.

He searched for a set of keys, but didn't find one. He supposed not all of them carried keys. Jack left William in the dust near the Wildman. The bears could have them both.

As he walked back to the fortress, he kept an eye on the two Jacks on the wall. There would be questions to answer. He already had a lot of the answers swirling in his head.

The Jacks could take the fortress from the Williams. Together with the Simples and the women, they would live happier lives. Lives without being told what to do every moment of the day. They would eat well without the Williams hoarding half the food.

Thinking of food made him think of the gardens. Jack vowed to never bury another body there. They would use the animal waste or food scraps—whatever else they could find. They wouldn't feast on crops raised from rotting Williams, the bears would. And if the bears grew stronger, they would shoot the bears. Bears made good food too. Jack smiled as he jogged to the fortress.

The door was open. He went in and was met by the two Jacks from the wall and the other that was on duty. At least they'd not summoned a William yet.

"What just happened out there? Jack-five says you killed a William. Explain yourself."

Jack did. He told them what William-four, the Simple, and the women had said. The other Jacks wore deep scowls by the time he finished.

"We'll remove the Williams and end this," he said.

Jack-five nodded. "Let's be done with them and cleanse our numbers."

They summoned their sleeping brothers.

William-nine approached the gathering Jacks with a stern face, the thin wisps of his blond hair standing on end in the gentle breeze. "What are you doing here? Why aren't you on the walls? And you, you're supposed to be resting."

Jack did a quick head count, they were missing one. "Where's Jack-three?"

William cocked his head. "He's in the vault on reward leave."

That figured. He hoped Jack-three was enjoying himself while all the chaos was going on above ground.

They had enough Jacks to carry out his plan without him. There would be time to give him the full story later.

He nodded to the two Jacks standing beside William-nine. They grabbed the fat man.

"Let me go. Get your hands off me. What the hell are you doing?"

Jack-five hit the William in the head. That

seemed to shut him up. They marched the stunned fat man toward the jail. No need to kill all the Williams just yet. He figured they'd need a few of them to answer questions for a while until the Jacks got the running of the fortress figured out.

"If the Williams give you too much trouble, kill them. Otherwise, bring them to the jail. Go."

He waved the Jacks off. The men dispersed, three heading back to the walls and the others heading toward the homes of the Williams. He went to the vault, intending to take out the William at the door.

When he got there, however, he didn't find anyone at the post. The chair was empty and the door stood ajar. Curious, Jack wandered inside, passing two open doors before pausing. A body lay on the floor. A big one. A William. His bloody stomach and chest were still. The women had said they'd attacked a William. He shrugged. That explained why there wasn't one at the door. This one didn't have keys either.

He went back to the top and pulled the door closed behind him. Until he found a set of keys for himself, he'd have to leave it unlocked. If the vault needed to be locked. From what he'd heard of the Wildman's confession, those poor fools didn't have much left in them.

Would the fortress fall to ruin without the help of the Williams? Part of him said no, but a tiny nagging voice kept telling him, yes.

Even as a small child on his mother's lap, he'd

been raised to listen to the Williams and Isaiahs, to do as they said and not question orders. Isaiahs studied the books, made plans, and fixed things. Williams led the fortress. Jacks kept them all safe and the Simples did the rest of the work. That was the way the fortress operated. It had worked that way for generations, and now he was changing things. His changes. Anything that went wrong would be his fault. And if he was wrong, would the other Jacks demand his life?

He hoped they would be of the same mind as he was. They acted like they were, but it was hard to tell now that he couldn't see them. Now that he was alone with his thoughts and the echoes of his footsteps, everything seemed so uncertain.

He made his way through the fortress to the rows of William houses, where he joined the others. The Jacks moved from door to door, pulling Williams who didn't resist, to the jail. The rest gathered bodies, exterminating the Williams with the efficiency they were all raised on thanks to the very same men they were killing—those men who controlled all but offered nothing. They deserved no part in the future of the fortress.

How many Williams were there? Jack wasn't sure. He couldn't ever remember seeing all of them together at one time to get an accurate count. In fact, he couldn't even bring all their faces to mind. When he tried, they melded together. Only the few with distinctive features stood apart from the rest. The one with three chins, the one whose cheeks were always red, the one who wheezed and breathed only through his mouth and the one with the big brown splotch on his forehead. It didn't matter, they'd find them all. A few might be out on duty, but they'd all turn up within a shift change.

He'd sent a handful of Williams off to the jail with four of the Jacks. The rest who were still living cowered on their knees in the dirt before him.

"Take three. Not too far, keep them within range so we can get a shot in at anything that comes to feed off them. Take the rest to the jail with the others for now. There are only so many bears we can eat and preserve at a time. If we cut the Williams' rations, we can keep them alive for awhile. We don't want to waste them."

The remaining Jacks nodded.

"One of you go see to the Simples."

"And what should we do with them? They get upset over the littlest thing. You think they won't be upset about this?"

"Nevermind, I'll talk to them. After hearing this Joshua, I think I have an idea of what will make them understand and be happy with the new situation. Get them all together and send them to the dining hall."

The Jacks went off to follow his orders. It surprised him at first that the Jacks would be so eager to do so, but then he realized that they'd been taking orders all their lives. The only difference now was that he was giving them instead of a William.

He looked around, discovering nothing looked quite the same as it had that morning. He went into the nearest William house. A bed, a nice bed compared to the one he had in the bunkhouse, sat against one wall. Opposite the bed were two doors. He opened one to find a bathroom. Just big enough for a toilet, shower, and sink. But to have a bathroom of his own would be very welcome. The bathroom the Jack's shared could only be accessed by going outside and around the back of their bunkhouse. And that only contained a single shower, toilet, urinal and two sinks.

With a bathroom of his own, he'd never have to wait for the shower or the toilet. No more baskets to hold his few personal things. He'd have a drawer and his own counter space. Jack grinned.

Behind the other door was a closet. The rainbow of shirts made him grimace, but as much as he preferred the simplicity of the coveralls all the Jack's wore, the fabric was heavy and coarse and very warm during hours under the sun. What fit a William's roll-filled arms, also would fit the muscles of a Jack. He unzipped his coverall and pulled a soft shirt over his arms and across his chest. The buttons took some getting used to, but he liked the smooth feel of the cloth. He tried on a pair of tan pants from the shelf. All the Williams seemed fond of that color. Maybe it was the only color the pants of their size were made. They fell right off his hips and didn't even come near his ankles.

Jack sighed as he pulled is coveralls back on, tying them up around his waist by the sleeves. He'd have to do some salvaging of the stores or elsewhere to find pants that would fit a Jack's body. No more uniforms.

He looked around the house, finding a book on the desk by the bed. The breeding book. William-fourteen's house.

How many times had he come here and been kept waiting by William's little power games? He snarled just thinking about it. Hopefully, that particular William wasn't one of the ones sitting in jail. He'd make a fine meal for a bear.

Jack sat down at the desk and ran his fingers over the worn, brown leather cover. The corners were cracked and darkened from all the fingers that had opened it over many years. Inside he found pages of printed lines filled with an assortment of written information, rows of names and dates and symbols in columns.

His reading skills weren't as good as a William's but he knew enough to see that the names in the beginning pages were many. Names he'd never heard of, like Harry, Nickolas, and Gerald. Hundreds of names he didn't know, people he'd never met. These men were the ones who had bred him to be who he was today. Men who were long dead, bones deep underground.

The ones who had first come to the fortress, when it was just a city block. That was the story the Williams told. They'd brought Simples from all around to research why they didn't get sick like most everyone else. They'd tested the food they ate, their genes, the bacteria in their stomachs, their brains, everything about their bodies, but most of the researchers died before they found answers, both from the virus and from the men who raided the buildings for food and supplies. The research was set aside while the area was reinforced. Buildings were torn down, walls erected, and food planted. The fortress was born.

He could see those same walls through the window. He would make sure they stood and that the work continued.

While there seemed to be numbers associated with the early names, later, the names vanished, and only numbers marked the new lives. He tried to follow the patterns, the scribbled notes of Isaiahs and others who left no name on their notations. The one thing that struck him was how often Simples had high numbers, often reaching four hundred before beginning again, where the other names only reached fifty before returning to one. There was one thing the Williams were right about, they were outnumbered.

Even more outnumbered were the women, right from the beginning of the book. While there were many different women's names at first, they quickly became breeder numbers. And so many of them only produced two or three children before a heavy line ran through their entry.

He wondered if they lived with the men or down in the vault-like they did now? Maybe they once lived in these very same houses. He could make that happen again. Without the Williams, extra able-bodied hands would be quite useful, and not having to worry about scavenging for comforts to keep them content would mean more time to focus on growing food and maintaining the buildings.

There were other longhouses, like those were the Jacks lived, deserted now, but that could be made livable again with minimal work. He stroked his stubbled chin and gave the idea some thought.

If the Simple and the women he'd taken with him did actually reach the Wildmen, the dirty raiders would have what they'd wanted all along. There would be no need to come back to his walls. Except for food, but that was a commodity he would be willing to trade if it meant not having to send Simples out on patrols as often or keep as many Jacks on the walls.

He would keep the skilled Simples busy doing some of the easier tasks Jacks usually performed. They liked having tasks, it kept their minds occupied so they didn't act out or get upset as often. Jack considered what he'd learned in dealing with Joshua. He'd seemed rather proud of his name. Maybe the others deserved their own as well. The Jacks too.

He needed to make life inside the fortress safe and more pleasant for all of them. If all went well, he'd have an increased population. And his would be healthier and better fed. Jack caught his reflection in the cracked mirror above the sink in the bathroom and smiled.

CHAPTER ELEVEN

Joshua checked the direction of the sun and led the others through the waist-high grass, mindful for snakes, rocks, and holes—all things Jacks had taught him to watch for when they were out scavenging. The sun had passed overhead and started downward by the time broken bits of old buildings faded into grasslands. This was where the city ended. He wasn't sure what city meant exactly, but he'd seen pictures of lots of buildings close together in a book once and a Jack had told him that was what it was.

Grasslands gave way to a path, spotted with clumps of grass rather than the flowing field behind and alongside him. His shoes scraped against a rough surface. Relief rushed through him. Pathways led to places. They weren't wandering anymore. They were going somewhere.

Every now and then he peered over his shoulder to make sure no Jacks were following them. But they were alone. He would have felt better if he'd had a map like the Jacks used. Even though he didn't know how to read it, the women might. They were smart. Except they were also busy carrying all the supplies and the tired and crying children.

That made him think of carrying Phillip and pulling Jack. His throat closed and he wanted to sit down and cry. But he couldn't do that, not with the mothers watching. He needed to be strong like a Jack. Jacks didn't cry.

Instead, he stopped walking and said, "We'll rest here." He didn't wait to see if they listened. He just sat on the path. The others sat too, putting down their supplies and children. The quiet sounds of mothers talking to the children and each other reminded him of his childhood. It was a safe sound. A happy one. His body ached, but inside he was warm and safe.

Susan, the dark-haired mother, came over and sat beside him. She handed him a thick piece of bread with chicken on it. He gobbled it down before he remembered to say thank you.

When he did, she wasn't mad. She smiled. Flecks of blood stuck to her face and hands, but Joshua decided she was still pretty. He smiled back.

"The others are scared here," she said.

A gentle wind blew through the stalks, rustling them together. In the distance, birds chirped and grasshoppers hummed. The mothers sat huddled together with their children held close. Some of the children slept, but the women stared at the grass clumps that stood just over their heads as if waiting for something to jump out and attack them.

"There are snakes in the grass, but most of them won't hurt you. That is why we walk on the path. It makes them easier to see, so we don't hurt them either. Stepping on them makes them angry."

Susan's smile faded. "We've never seen such a big place before. It's so...open."

"I miss the walls and the Jacks, but I like this too," he said.

"You've been out here before?" She moved closer, until she was right beside him, her arm almost touching his.

Joshua nodded. "Williams send us out to find treasures for you."

She smiled again, making his insides feel all warm. "We don't need treasures, but we would like walls, somewhere we can feel safe."

"The Wildmen will make us safe."

Susan took his hand in hers. Joshua gulped.

"Madeline, Emelda, and I have been talking. We're not so sure that Phillip's people will be as happy to see us as he said they would, especially since he's not with us now. Maybe we should find somewhere safe first. We can go find them when we're better prepared."

He wasn't sure what Susan meant exactly, but he wanted her to keep holding his hand so he nodded. "We'll go west. We can go north later."

"Thank you, Joshua." She squeezed his hand and let go.

Susan went back over to her friends. The three of them gathered their own children and got everyone else on their feet. They all looked to Joshua. He checked the sun and left the path to aim west.

By nightfall, they'd found another path that headed the right direction. He wasn't able to give them four walls for the night, but he did find a building alongside the path that had most of three walls and half a roof.

His followers stood outside, watching the moon creep over the horizon and the stars twinkle. They didn't look scared again until he told them to go inside and get to sleep. He made sure to lie down between them and the open wall. Their nervous whispers finally settled down.

He woke to a snorting, grunting sound he knew too well from his patrol runs. A bear.

Fear gripped him so hard he couldn't move. Jacks always carried a gun when they left the fortress. He didn't have any weapons. Nothing but his hands.

He watched as it grabbed a bundle that someone had left outside. It pawed at the fabric with its long claws, shredding it in seconds. The bear shoved its snout into the mess and found something to eat.

Slowly remembering William-four's lessons, Joshua got to his feet and crept backward, waking the others as he went.

"Stand together and be quiet," he whispered. "Don't run. Bears like runners." Joshua made his way back to the front of the group to find the bear watching them.

A stink, like every dog in the kennel had gotten wet and then rolled in week old kitchen scraps, wafted toward him. The bear huffed, like the William who had made him carry Jack out of the vault. It reared up on its hind legs and let out a growl that made Joshua shiver from head to foot.

Children cried. Women whimpered. But no one ran. Joshua was pretty sure he couldn't have moved if he wanted to. He wasn't even sure where his feet were. All he knew was the big, hairy bear glaring at him with moonlight glinting in its eyes.

Susan's soft voice squeaked as she said, "Joshua."

He couldn't let the bear hurt anyone. They needed him to protect them. He had to be a Jack even though he had no gun. Joshua closed his eyes and searched for the brave, strong voice inside him.

The bear snorted and let out another fierce growl. One of the women screamed. Hands grabbed at the back of his shirt and bodies pressed close, both big and small. The scent of the vault surrounded him.

Joshua opened his eyes, raised his arms and spread them wide. He yelled as loud as he could, louder than he'd ever heard a William yell.

The bear dropped to the ground on all four legs with a loud thump. It shook its head and growled again. Joshua's heart beat so fast that he thought it might pop right out of his chest.

The bear snorted, turned around, and then lumbered off in the direction from which they'd come.

Positive he'd never sleep again and grateful he'd not peed his pants, Joshua turned to the others and declared that they would walk until they found a better place to stay. No one argued.

The night sky had faded to a dusky gray when the rain began to fall. The cracked path spread out ahead of them, promising to lead them somewhere—eventually.

Joshua called them to a rest under a stand of trees. The leaves blocked the worst of the weather, but water dripped down their faces like tears and soaked their clothes. The mothers wrapped their children in wet blankets and pulled them onto their wet skirts. They huddled together, shivering, teeth chattering and staring into the trees as if another bear might appear at any moment.

Watching the mothers, he found his gaze glued to all the curves the clinging fabric revealed. He'd never given much thought to the things about women he'd overheard when Jacks met on the pathways or in the dining hall. But now that he was surrounded by women it started to make sense.

His mouth went dry as he considered what the Williams preached about the women. They were treasures because they made babies. They needed Jacks to make the babies. He was the Jack now. And there were a lot of women. And he didn't even know how to make babies beyond what he'd seen Jack doing to Arianne.

Even worse, these women were scared. And tired. And all their supplies were wet. And he didn't know where they were or how long it would be before they found a better place to sleep than the one the night before. Jacks never looked scared when they traveled outside the fortress and that had made him feel okay about being outside the walls. As much as he wanted to crush his knees to his chest and curl up between the giant roots of the tree he was leaning against, he couldn't look scared.

When he'd imagined leading the girls to freedom, this wasn't at all what he'd pictured. Phillip was supposed to be here, showing him what to do and where to go. A lump formed in his throat. He wasn't supposed to be out here by himself.

Susan approached him with a little girl in one hand and a little boy peeking around her skirt. "The rain seems to be stopping."

The grey clouds didn't look much lighter to him, but they did have to keep moving. Spending the night out in the open would only make them more scared, and he really did need to sleep. They all did.

Joshua stretched his aching muscles. One of the nurse mothers ran over to him with a young child in her arms. Red blotches and blisters covered one of the boy's arms from his elbow to his hand.

"What is this?" she asked, holding his arms apart. "Can you fix it?"

The boy struggled to get his other hand free and cried when he couldn't break her hold on his wrist. Other mothers gathered around, children in their arms. As they pulled up sleeves and pants and skirts, checking all the other children, their conversation grew more frantic, like his friends when they were upset, their voices getting higher and louder until he thought they might all start crying as loud as the little boy.

"My mother was right," said Miranda. "They're catching the virus. We're all going to—"

Joshua held up his hands like Williams did when trying to calm his friends, and tried to keep his voice calm. "That's from a plant. It's just itchy."

Really itchy, as he recalled. The bad plant sometimes grew in the little-used places in the fortress. When Williams sent him and his friends in to clean those places out, one or two of them often ended up with the itchy red blisters. The Williams kept a little plot of a plant with orange flowers that made the itch go away. But he didn't have the plot of flowers to run to. He'd have to find them. Somewhere.

"We should go." He couldn't remember what the bad plant looked like, but it was here somewhere and the longer they stayed, the more of a chance of others touching it.

"Try not to itch. It will take longer to get better if you do."

With both mothers and children crying and miserable, and a light drizzle still falling, they again set out on the path. Some walked with halting steps, and others muttered under their breath. He wondered if they wished they were back in the fortress.

The sun floated only two hands above the horizon when the outlines of buildings beckoned to them from in the distance. Joshua wanted to run, but the others couldn't muster anything beyond a brisk walk that even a William could have kept up with.

Trying to make them move faster, he gathered up the supplies that three of the women were carrying and wrapped them into one of the blankets another carried. He slung the bulky lump over his back and tied it across his chest. Then, with a squalling child in each arm, he led them onward.

By the time the sun was nothing more than a swiftly sinking arc of orange, they finally reached the buildings. Joshua's stomach dropped to his feet. All the windows and doors were broken or gone and the roofs sagged in the middle or had branches growing through them. Vines grew up the sides, feeling their way inside and exploring the rooms. Jacks wouldn't let them into these buildings. Holes in the roof meant rain inside and that made the floor soft. Soft floors could break legs or worse.

"We have to sleep outside," he announced.

No one had energy to complain. He chose a spot covered with low growing plants so they could at least see if a bear or something even worse came around. They dropped their supplies. Those that had blankets, damp as they were, spread them out and curled up beside their children. They all grew silent.

Joshua tried to keep his eyes open, but his eyelids were so heavy. By the third time his chin hit his chest, he gave up. He didn't even bother to unwrap his bundle to use the blanket. That required more energy than he had left. Joshua lay down in the weeds and slept.

CHAPTER TWELVE

William-eleven stared at the body of William-fourteen, sprawled across the floor beside the desk, as he was marched into the jail. How would they ever replace him? He was the only one who had understood the old Isaiah's meandering notes. He'd been assisting Isaiah since he'd left the vault as a child. None of the young Williams they'd tried to give him as an apprentice over the years had met with William-fourteen's approval. Now they had no one.

The Jack behind him rammed his rifle into William's back. "I said, move."

"You will bury him, right? He's served us all long and well." He wished he'd had a chance to see which of the hot-headed idiots had killed William-fourteen. He'd save him a special punishment.

"Six said we're to feed the dead to the bears. Sounds a lot easier than digging a hole big enough for that one."

William-eleven gasped. The stench of loosened bowels filled his nose. "You can't do that."

"You don't get to tell us what we can and can't do anymore, fat man. There might be more of you than us, but not for long."

He walked deeper into the jail, trying to breathe through his mouth. His fingers wrapped around the ring of keys in the pocket of his pants. If he was lucky, the Jack would lock him in and forget to take them. He would be free as soon as he had a moment alone. He could fix this, get the fortress back under control. All he had to do was gather the other Williams together and get the horde of Simples to protect them from the Jacks. As long as the Jacks didn't use their guns. William grimaced, imagining the chaos of Simples running from gunfire, leaving Williams easy targets.

How many Simples and Williams would have to die to regain control of the fortress? They'd put the younger Williams in with the Simples. The wealth of knowledge held by the older William's was irreplaceable. They would hide. And the Simples? He shrugged. There were plenty of them to spare.

The Jack shoved him against the bars of the first cell, pressing his cheeks into the metal as he patted down William's shirt and then his pants. He removed the keys and shoved William inside.

He slammed into the stone wall at the back of the cell, smashing his nose against the rock and cutting open his chin. Blood filled his mouth. When he spit it out, one of his front teeth floated in the bloody glob. His eyes watered so hard he couldn't get a clear view of the Jack before he shut the door with a heavy clank, closed the lock, and left.

He unbuttoned his shirt and pulled it off. Using

his favorite light blue shirt, he applied pressure to his nose and chin. It was ruined anyway with all the blood splatters.

The blood had stopped flowing and a steady throbbing had taken hold of his face when Jack-two, one of the youngest of the Jacks, entered with William-fifteen.

Blond stubble edged Jack's chin and cheeks and his eyes were alight with a determined gleam. "Got a pal for you."

Jack-two tossed red-faced William-fifteen into the cell across from William-eleven. Within twenty minutes, three more Williams filled three more cells.

To William-eleven's dismay, none of the other Williams held positions that required keys. Getting out the easy way wasn't an option.

He let out a heavy sigh. "What's gotten into the Jacks? Did they give any of you an indication?"

William-fifteen rubbed his perpetually red cheeks and paced his cell. "This is chaos." He wrinkled his nose. "And the smell—"

"William-fourteen is dead," William said.

"They were dragging him out when Jack-six brought me in," said one of the other Williams, from further down the row.

"Then why does it still smell so bad?"

"Another body?" suggested William-sixteen.

"Oh yes, there's someone down here. Looks like a Jack's coverall."

"Well, well," said William-eleven, "That means there's only nine of them left." He gripped the cold, steel bars and shook them but nothing happened. He knew the jail was secure and the repairs up to date. It had to be in case it had to hold Jacks. And if the cell could contain a Jack, it could certainly contain him.

"The next time they bring another of us in, we'll signal him to slip us his keys or try to grab ours from the Jack as he passes by."

"You really think it would be that easy?" asked William-fifteen.

"Jacks aren't smart."

"They figured out how to drag us off to jail pretty easily."

"They did use the element of surprise and they're stronger than us. We've been cautious of that from the beginning," said one of the other Williams.

"Not cautious enough." William-eleven leaned his back against the bars, waiting.

No one came in. No noise from outside. After awhile, his legs began to hurt. He slumped down on the floor.

Nothing made sense. He rubbed his hands over his face. Where had they gone wrong? Where did the Jacks even get the idea to revolt, let alone the motivation to do so? They'd tried so hard to keep the Jacks in line by directing their ambitions toward protecting the women and their aggressions toward the Wildmen. It had worked for generations.

Did the Jacks realize that they needed the Simples for labor or would they get rid of them as competition for food and mates? They could afford to lose most of the Simples, but some were needed for food production, scavenging, tending what little livestock they had and maintaining the fortress itself. Without them, life as they knew it would come to a sudden halt. The Jacks knew nothing beyond fighting and sex. That's what they were bred for. They certainly weren't the brains of the overall mission. William bit his lip, wondering what was changing in the world outside the jail and how it would affect him after he managed to get out.

There would be hell to pay. That was for sure. Whichever Jack had infected the others with this seed of revolution would need to be put down. He hoped it wouldn't be more than one Jack. Their muscle was necessary to keep the Wildmen at bay. Though, he pondered, from what he'd heard from the interrogation of the Wildman prisoner, their losses had been heavy. They might be able to thin the Jacks a little more and not suffer dearly for it.

How could they have missed the signs of a rebel in the making? Jacks weren't known for subterfuge. They wore their thoughts on their faces—serious, sad and angry. There wasn't much in between. Satisfied—usually after the week of their mating time, but that wore off within days. Then they went back to brooding and the rest. Would this wear off too? Would the Jacks come to their senses and realize that they needed the Williams? He hoped so.

The bars pressed into his back. He shifted, but couldn't find a comfortable position on the hard floor. His legs hurt, his back ached, and he was pretty sure his nose was broken.

Damn Jacks. Tiny brains in big bodies. Why hadn't they managed to breed that out of them? Why not a single Jack with the mind of an Isaiah? Of all the lines to dry up, why was it the one they needed most?

He would try to reason with the next Jack to enter. He'd had a lot of practice with that. He could do it again. Jacks responded well to the right kind of coercion. They were too dim to realize that they were being manipulated just as much as the Simples. The only reason they were given some power over the Simples was to keep them happy and give them the illusion that they were a step up.

William sat and waited. Hours passed. Finally, the door banged open.

A young William was led by Jack-six. A gash lined the boy's forehead. William-eleven recognized him as the one who'd been stationed in the barn, overseeing the Simples who tended the livestock. He was only ten, so young, William-eleven hadn't been around him enough to memorize his number. With all the health problems that plagued the Williams, he often didn't bother until they reached fifteen. Too many of them died.

He tried to signal the boy, but he couldn't catch his eye. The young William trembled and blubbered and begged for his freedom. His training had fallen apart. Nothing about him would make a Jack stop his actions and respect the boy's authority.

William-eleven pulled himself to his feet. "Stop there. Explain the meaning of this."

Jack-six stormed by as if they'd not even heard him. Keys clanged against the metal bars. The door squeaked. "Your youth saved you. Remember that when we ask you to be useful," he said.

"Jack-six. I am speaking to you. You will answer my question."

Jack-six spun around to face him. "I don't recall you asking a question."

"Explain what is going on. And why are you out of uniform? Why are you wearing a William's shirt?"

"You're no longer in control. That's what's going on. No more babies in the garden. No more stockpiles of food. No more Williams." He started for the door.

"Wait! You can't kill us. You need us." William hated that he sounded rather sniveling and far too much like the boy William.

"We need some of you. For now. That's why you're here and not outside the walls like the other Williams who were...less cooperative."

William drew a deep breath and killed the snide comment on his tongue. Better to calm the savage beast than antagonize it. "How can we help?"

"You'll instruct the Simples and all the other children now that they are no longer in the vault. You'll teach them our history and direct them into our future. But you won't rule them. You'll serve them. Like we've all served you for too long. You'll eat what you're given and you'll speak when you're directed to. If you don't like your new role, we'll be looking for more bear bait in a few weeks." Jack-six offered him a flat smile that did nothing to ease his nerves. "Stocking up on meat for winter."

William cringed inwardly. "You're letting the women and children out of the vault?"

"Should have been done a long time ago. They can work for their food like the rest of us."

"But what about the breeding program?"

Jack laughed. "Have you seen the men in the fortress? Have you seen how your breeding program has worked for us? You and the Isaiah's have carefully guided us straight into a dead end."

They were going to disregard everything their ancestors had worked so hard for. William felt his composure crumble. His face fell. He knew it did. He saw the reflection of his failure in the Jack's eyes. A sad man with a round face and a brown birthmark marring his forehead.

There had to be a way he could minimize the damage. "And how do you plan to correct our mistake, Jack? You can't understand the book. Most Williams couldn't even understand it. Let me take a look. Maybe I can help."

Jack shook his head. "It's just a bunch of names of men who no longer exist. Names of the last men to bear our resemblance, a Jack, a William and an Isaiah. You've shoved us into molds to keep your precious order, but all your work has gotten us nowhere. I think it's time for a little chaos."

William sagged against the bars.

Jack-six surveyed the other Williams. "You'll all pick a name." He shot William-eleven a narrow-eyed scowl. "Not William. I'll need to know how each of you can be useful to the fortress. Sitting idly in a chair and yelling at Simples is no longer an option. We'll begin in the morning. I expect your names and uses then."

"What about food? When will we eat?" asked the youngest William.

"You'll survive." Jack peered past the boy into the dim light provided by the narrow windows at the rear of the cells just below the roofline. "Three, is that you?"

He crept closer, and finding the cell door open, went inside. He rushed out seconds later, spinning around in the midst of the occupied cells. "You've killed my brother. I needed him. How could you do this?"

Jack had killed his brothers too, William wanted to scream at him but kept his mouth shut. Clearly, this Jack was in charge and not against losing another William or two. He had no desire to meet a bear firsthand.

When no one answered him, Jack stormed out of the jail, slamming the door shut behind him.

William sank to the floor. "Did any of you know about Jack-three?"

They shook their heads. Silence and the stench of death settled over them all.

William started to sweat. The cell was too small. He needed sunlight. He needed fresh air. He licked his dry lips.

"We have to get out of here. What did you see

before they brought you?" he asked the boy.

His voice shook. "Jacks were patrolling the interior like it was the wall or the paths outside. They checked each building before they came to the barn where I was watching them. I expected them to give me a report, thinking one of you had ordered them to search for something, but as soon as they caught sight of me, they grabbed me and brought me here."

"What about the other Williams?"

His voice shook even more. "I saw a pair of Jacks carrying a William between them. They were heading for the east door."

"Did he say anything to you? Give you any sign of what was going on?"

"He didn't answer me when I yelled to him. I think he was unconscious."

An unconscious man would have no defense against the beasts that prowled the darkness of night. They'd only find his remains in the morning.

"What about the Simples?"

"Didn't see a single one. One of the Jacks said something about gathering them up in the dining hall."

"What were they going to do with them?" asked the red-faced William.

"Your guess is as good as mine."

William groaned. "The women?"

"I heard some left with a Simple calling himself Joshua. The rest were still in the vault as far as I know."

"Women left with a Simple? Out into the wild

lands?" William slumped to the floor.

"What are we going to do?"

"Wait. Nothing else we can do."

"Do you think they'll set us free if we cooperate?" the boy asked.

"Why wouldn't they?" asked the red-faced William.

William thought about what the Jack had said and how many pieces he'd like to tear the man into. "Because, sadly, they're smart enough not to."

CHAPTER THIRTEEN

Two days after they'd left the skeletons of houses behind, Joshua spotted another row of buildings on the horizon. Susan's boy, sitting on Joshua's shoulders, kicked his feet against Joshua's chest.

"Look, look," the boy chanted until Joshua's ears were just as annoyed as the muscles on his chest.

He put the boy down, deciding it would be better to walk slower than make Susan angry by throwing him into the grass beside the path. As he set the boy on his feet, Joshua saw the one thing he'd been searching for. Orange flowers. A whole cluster of the same plants the Williams used. He darted into the grass to pluck a handful of the long-stemmed plants from the ground. The group stopped, staring at him, as he held his treasure up high.

"Rub the juice on your rash. It will make the itch stop." As he handed Susan the first bunch and reached for more, a sparkle caught his attention. Water.

Joshua handed Susan another handful of flowered stems before moving through the plants to the little stream that came from the trees and curved toward the buildings ahead. He knelt down beside the rocky edge and scooped up a handful of chilly, clear water. The sweet taste of good water made his tongue dance. He never wanted to have to lick dew off leaves again. This tasted so much better. He drank another handful before standing and calling the rest of the group over.

The mothers and children trampled the grass and the remaining plants. Their complaining and crying turned to slurping and splashing.

With water-laden bellies, they rushed toward the buildings. The hope of a roof over their heads made even the young children walk faster. Excited chatter followed close behind as Joshua led the way.

By dusk they'd reached what turned out to be the remnants of houses, their walls leaning inward and roofs caved in. Excitement turned to despair. The stream veered away as if even it had given up on this place.

"Don't worry. This is a big place. We'll find somewhere to rest," he said.

The mothers nodded, but their faces were tired and their eyes said they didn't believe him.

Thick trees lined the path that branched off into other paths. More buildings than he could count surrounded them, so many he couldn't see them all. One of them had to be safe enough for his people.

Joshua paused. His people. He grinned.

"Wait here. I'll look around," he said.

Susan, Emelda, and Madeline talked to one another for a moment. Passing their children to

Madeline, Susan and Emelda came over to join him.

"We'll go with. No one should go off alone," Emelda said.

That was one of the rules when he went scavenging, but he hadn't expected that any of them would want to go with him; exploring was a job for Simples and Jacks. He looked at the two pretty mothers and nodded. Not being alone made him feel braver. He liked that. He couldn't be scared if they came with him.

Leaving the others behind, Joshua chose one of the paths and started down it. Susan and Emelda walked beside him, looking at everything as they walked and asking what things were. He did his best to answer them, even though their questions and looking slowed him down.

Joshua checked the sinking sun yet again and walked faster, hoping that walking farther ahead of the mothers would keep them from talking as much.

In a big space without any buildings, stood posts, twists of metal, and tall metal rods, from which long, rusted chains hung in pairs. Strange formations of metal grids formed a framework for flowering vines and other plants. Blackberries filled bushes. The familiar sight of them made his mouth water. "We can eat these," he announced.

Joshua took a handful for himself and stepped back to let Susan and Emelda have a turn. He popped the slightly sour berries into his mouth, one by one, savoring the tangy juice.

"Remember where this is so we can tell the

others," Susan told Joshua.

"I will. We need to find a building made of bricks. Those are safer." He scanned the buildings along the path.

"Like that one?" asked Susan, pointing to a house with vines covering the roof and brown bricks along the bottom half of the front wall.

"No, big bricks. Grey ones." He led them down the path and onto two others before he came to a building the size of many houses put together.

Most of the windows were gone and the door hung askew, but the walls were straight and the roof looked whole.

Darkness loomed. Joshua climbed the stone steps and peered into the shadows outside the building. Nothing that looked like a bear jumped out at him. But they could be waiting inside.

He took a deep breath and faced the darkness through the doorway. "I need to make sure it's safe. Wait out here." He stepped in. The floor squeaked with each step but seemed solid enough. It didn't groan or shatter like some of the old unsafe places did in the fortress.

Taking a deep breath, he yelled, "Anything in here?" His heart pounded as he waited, straining to hear the sound of claws on the floor, growling, roaring or anything else that would mean he had to run away fast. But there was only silence.

Joshua ran back outside. "This will work. We need to get the others before it's too dark to find our way back."

Suddenly, he wasn't tired or sore anymore. He had to keep waiting for Susan and Emelda. "Hurry," he told them again and again until they started to look angry.

When they finally reached the others, he told them what they'd found. The mothers quickly gathered up their bundles and their children. With only a few pricked fingers and complaints of scratches from thorns, they filled their hands with berries. Then they moved on, eating along the way as Joshua brought them to the place he'd found.

Standing on the stone steps, he gave the mothers and children the same warning Jacks did when they entered a new place. "Stay together and be careful." He backed into the doorway. "I'll go first, follow one by one. Walk where I walk."

Inside a few more steps than he'd ventured before, he felt around, bumping into several hard things of varying heights, but it was too dark to tell what they were. Despite the obstacles, the space seemed big enough for all of them. At least they'd be safe and dry.

A hand brushed against his back, and the sound of shuffling feet filled the room. Mothers called out to one another. Grunts exploded as others bumped into the same obstacles he had. A baby cried.

"Is everyone inside?" he asked.

Madeline answered. "Yes, I was the last one in."

"Good. Sit where you are and sleep. Don't go in farther until we can see better."

Brick buildings might be safer, but they were still

old and not being able to see well enough to explore properly made him nervous.

He hoped the pointy bits of the broken windows he'd seen earlier would keep any animals away, but the door needed to close. Joshua felt his way back to the sliver-of-a-moonlit doorway and pulled on it. He tugged on it. He yanked on it until his shoulders hurt. Finally, the old hinges agreed to work. It wouldn't latch, but it did close.

Safe inside the building, they slept.

Joshua dreamed of patrol runs that never ended, and bears that talked to him with the voice of Williams. Phillip stood next to Jack-three and smiled at him. Jack told him not to listen to the bear. He walked and walked until his legs shook and then Susan was there holding his hand.

Sunlight tickled his eyelids. Joshua opened them to find the soft morning light chasing the night's shadows from his new surroundings. Women and children stood in front of the broken glass, staring at the rising sun. He stretched, got to his feet and went to join them.

Susan came to stand beside him. "It's so beautiful."

The rising sun meant it was time to get up and get to work. It meant another day of stacking bricks, or working in the garden or running the patrol paths outside the walls. None of that was beautiful. Beautiful was dandelion seeds dancing on the breeze or a puppy curled up on his lap or...Susan smiling beside him with the soft light of the morning sun on her face.

"Yes," he said.

The others began to mill about, reminding him that he had to make sure the rest of the room was safe before he went out to look for something other than berries to fill their stomachs.

The things he'd bumped into the night before turned out to be shelves filled with rows of books. Lots of shelves. All filled with books.

Small rooms, some with glass walls that revealed tables and chairs inside, stood along some of the outside walls. Two wide hallways led off from the big room where they'd slept. A long row of tables ran down the middle of the big room, some still topped with the black screens that Jack-three had once told him were computers. These even still had the cables running from the backs of them. No one had taken them yet to use for tying up plants or pants or pulled the wires out of the plastic to use for decorations or holding things together like the bottom of his bunk back at the fortress.

"There are so many," said Susan, running her hand over a dust-covered row of books covered with smooth paper in all different colors. "We can learn whatever we need to right here."

He sneezed. "Only touch what we need. It makes less dust in the air."

She spun around, laughing. "We need it all, Joshua. This library is perfect. Our new home."

"But we're not staying here. We're going to meet Phillip's people."

"We don't need them. Don't you see? We have everything we need here." She took his hand in hers. "And you."

His tongue tripped over words as he tried to think of how to explain why he needed to meet the Wildmen. He'd promised Phillip. Even though Susan and her friends had knives, they would all be safer with more men around to watch for animals and to hunt and to help make babies. He couldn't do all of that by himself, and the mothers had children to watch over. They couldn't help him all the time.

Joshua held Susan's hand. Looking down at his fingers wrapped around hers, he forgot what he was trying to say.

"You should take some of the others out to look for food. Show them how to look. Show them what to watch out for."

He slowly remembered: The mothers had children to watch and they'd need to teach them now that there were no Williams to do that. The mothers would need time to read these books to learn what to teach.

As much as he didn't want to, he took his hand from Susan's so he could think better again. "I'll show them how to find food, but we also need to find Phillip's people."

Susan turned to the mothers fussing with their children's hair or wiping dirty faces on their sleeves or skirts. "If you have to, then you should go."

Joshua's mouth fell open and it felt like the floor did too. "Me? You're coming too, aren't you? All of you?"

Susan took his hand. "A few of us can go with you, but not all. We don't know if it's safe. This is a good place. I like it here. Some of us should stay and read and learn so we'll be ready when you come back."

"Ready for what?"

"To either go with you or to make our home here." She wrapped her hand over his arm and gently led him away from the others. "The Wildmen have been trying to get into the fortress for a long time. What have they always wanted?"

"Food and women," he said quietly.

"Exactly. If you take all of us to them, what's to stop them from taking us from you? Even with our knives, the four of us wouldn't be near enough to protect the whole group from armed Wildmen. It's not safe for all of us to go. Do you understand?"

Joshua nodded. He didn't want the Wildmen to take any of his people. Ever. Especially not Susan.

She leaned in close and kissed his cheek. "I knew you would."

Joshua's face grew warm. He grinned and then his face grew even warmer when he realized the other women were watching him and giggling.

She shook her head and laughed at the others, then pushed him toward the door. "Go on. I'll send some women out to help you look for food."

He floated out of the library and down the stairs, unable to stop grinning. Three Simple women, Grace, and three older children joined him.

A cool morning breeze caressed his face, a cleaner, sweeter breeze than he'd ever felt inside the fortress walls. No outhouses or barns fouled the air. He breathed deep and tried not to think about going to see the Wildmen without all the women to make him brave.

Joshua did his best to teach his group like a William—but without the yelling and hitting. They learned which buildings were safe to try and which ones they should never go into. He showed them how to search and tried to explain what to look for. He also took them back to the place they'd found the berries and showed them which plants were food and which were just pretty to look at. They found a wagon in a little building behind one of the houses and filled it as they went.

They found containers to hold water and followed the main path back to where the stream flowed beside it. They returned to the library with their wagon full of water containers and the edible plants they'd found. After a quick meal, they set off again.

In the basement of one old house, they found four plastic tubs full of clothes of all different sizes. They were dry and clean and though they smelled musty, they held the promise of other treasures waiting to be discovered in this new place.

While the women were bringing two of the tubs up the stairs to the wagon, he rifled through another and found a shirt that went all the way to his hands and pants that went all the way to his feet. Not a threadbare spot to be found. No mended elbows or mismatched buttons. No blood stains. He quickly slipped them on. He emptied his pockets into the new ones. The pants sagged around his waist and threatened to slouch to his knees as he took an exploratory step. With regret, he slipped the rope he wore for a belt on his old pants into the loops of the new ones. He cinched it tight and took a few steps, marveling how the clean fabric felt on his skin. He was Joshua now, with no worn, handed down, ill-fitting clothes to mark him as a Simple. He ran to help the others carry the rest of their treasures back to the library.

"What's all this?" asked Susan as he began to unload the wagon.

"Clothes," said one of the children who had helped Joshua explore. He smiled proudly. "Our own clothes. Joshua says they've only been worn a few times before. Look how new they are." He pointed to Joshua.

Her gaze traveled from his shirt to his pants and back up again and then she smiled. "Very handsome. I can't wait to see what else is in there. These skirts and dresses," she nodded toward the other mothers, "aren't very practical for working, and we'll all need to work if we wish to make a home together."

Joshua's stomach fluttered. She was still looking at him like he'd done something wonderful. Her smiles were far better than a smile from a William. Hers made him warm inside, made him feel silly, like he wanted to laugh and wanted her to laugh with him. Maybe if he tickled her.

He brought one of the tubs up onto the stairs where Susan stood and handed it to one of the mothers waiting there. While she opened the lid and started pulling out clothes, Joshua reached for Susan's side. Before he could tickle her, she wrapped her arms around him and squeezed tight.

"Thank you, Joshua. You've done a wonderful job," she whispered in his ear.

In that moment, he no longer missed his mother. The ache within him was filled. He carefully put his arms around Susan, trying not to squeeze too tight or put his hands anywhere that might make her angry.

"You can let go now, Joshua," she said, laughing.

He stepped back quickly, arms dropping to his sides. Just as he was feeling as though he'd done something wrong, she took his hand and pulled him aside so the Simple mothers who had explored with him could bring the rest of the tubs into the library.

Inside, women and children crowded around the tubs, mothers holding up clothes to either children or themselves, passing items around until they all held at least one new thing.

The mothers, scattered throughout the library changed their children's clothes. When it came to changing their own, they gave him uncertain looks.

"Use the other rooms," said Susan. "We will all have to get used to new ways of doing things."

Madeline and Emelda helped bring the nurse mothers and Simples to rooms without glass walls so they could change out of sight.

Disappointment hung over Joshua. Seeing the other woman change would have given him a better idea of what was under all their clothes, of all the good parts Jacks talked about. His sullen mood quickly vanished when Susan exited one of the rooms and made her way to him.

Her legs were long and thin in pants instead of a skirt and her chest bounced under the tight shirt she wore as she walked. "This feels wonderful," she said, spinning around and laughing.

Joshua nodded. He tried to speak but found his voice gone. He cleared his throat and tried again. "Did you find good books while we were gone?"

"Great books. There is so much to learn." She grinned. "The children love the big space. They feel safer inside. They can run and play, which gave us all time to look around more. The Simples are also feeling more at ease."

"That's good," he said, basking in her grin and the safe feeling she gave him, and the others. Susan was just as smart as a William and almost as handy as a Jack with her knife. And she could read and teach and help make the food and give the others jobs without being bossy. She was far better than Jack-three's Muriel.

He bit his lip, feeling around in his pocket until his fingers located the small, cloth-wrapped bundle. "I have a present for you." He handed her the bundle.

Susan took it, and after looking at him for a long

moment, opened the cloth to reveal a wire wrapped blue stone on a cord. She held it up, the stone spinning around as it dangled in the air.

"It's beautiful. Thank you." She slipped the cord over her neck and kissed his cheek. "I'm glad I came. Otherwise, I never would have met you."

"I'm glad too."

She laughed, taking his hand and pulling him outside. They sat on the steps next to one another. "How long until you leave?" she asked.

"I will take them out again tomorrow and make sure they learned what I told them. Then I should go. Will you come with me?"

Susan glanced over her shoulder to look into the library. Children yelled, women talked, and feet marched over the floor.

"I think I should stay," she said quietly. "When you're not here, the others will need someone to help them feel safe."

Joshua stared at their hands on his lap. He needed someone to help him feel safe too. "I can't go by myself."

"No, I will find some volunteers to go with you, some of the women who wouldn't mind staying with the Wildmen, if it comes to that."

"I just want to talk to them. We can decide what to do when I get back."

"They might not be so friendly, Joshua. We don't have Phillip to talk to them for us."

Joshua sighed. Her hand slipped away from his, twisting together on her own lap.

"It will be all right, Joshua. You've done so well so far. Don't be afraid now."

But she was afraid. Her hands shook anytime they were still and she wouldn't look at him. He knew very well what afraid looked like. At least he wasn't afraid alone.

"I won't."

She stood. "I'll find your volunteers. You get some rest and then pack enough food and water for the journey. The others will pack for themselves." She strode to the doorway and then turned back to him. "You'll come see me before you leave, won't you?"

"Yes." He'd do anything she wanted if it meant she might kiss him again.

CHAPTER FOURTEEN

Jack-six stood at the front of the dining hall and looked over the host of Simples gathered at the tables. They mumbled amongst themselves, a few watching him, most avoiding his gaze as they usually did.

He cleared his throat. "I asked you to come here because there will be some changes around the fortress starting right now. First of all, you will no longer be taking orders from Williams. You will listen to Jacks. The Williams have been very bad and are being punished. If you find a William, tell a Jack right away. Got it?"

Their mouths hung open, but after a moment they uttered their agreement.

"Good. Do any of you remember the names you had when you were children?"

Most of them nodded. Some looked confused. This was the first step in implementing a big change for the Simples, and he wanted it to be special, to show them that Jacks weren't like Williams.

"If you can't remember it, we'll help you pick a name. But as of today, you are no longer numbers. You have a name. Use it. Tell your name to the Jacks you are working with. It might take us a while to learn all your names, but we'll try hard."

The Simples grinned.

"We'll be watching you, how you work, how well you follow instructions. Those of you who do a very good job will get to move into the building that we Jacks have used. You will get bigger beds and more space to yourselves. There is a real bathroom there with a shower."

Cheering filled the hall. They weren't used to rewards. In fact, Jack couldn't remember them ever getting a reward. He wanted to tell them about the possibility of having mates of their own, but he needed to talk to the women first. They should have a say too.

"We aren't going to ask you to do patrol runs outside the fortress anymore. Instead, you will walk the walls with Jacks. Guns will still be for Jacks but you can help watch. If you see something, tell the Jack on your wall right away, and he will take care of it. Can you do that?"

Some nodded enthusiastically and blurted out their eagerness to help. Others hunched their shoulders and lowered their heads as though they wished they could vanish. He'd have to be patient with them.

"Good. There will also be more food. The Williams were stealing from us. There is enough food for everyone. We will all eat here and get equal portions."

The Simples cheered and clapped, even the ones

who'd been quiet the moment before.

Jack was afraid that if he said anything else, they would be so excited they'd forget everything he'd already covered. "That's all for now. Remember, if you see a William, tell a Jack. Everyone who has a patrol shift, report to the walls instead and don't forget to tell us your names. You're dismissed."

With much excitement and chatter, the Simples dispersed.

Jack had never seen them cheer for a William. With a light step, he headed to the vault.

"I'm going to have a talk with the women, see if they're willing to join us up here," he said to Jack-two. "Make sure the rest of you keep an eye on the Simples. They'll have questions and some of them may need some guidance. Be patient. We don't want them scared of us."

The young man nodded and sprinted off to spread his instructions. He wondered if Two remembered his childhood name. It had been so long, he no longer remembered his own. Maybe he would stick with Jack, be the last one.

The seat at the vault door was vacant. For a moment it was unsettling to not see a William stationed there. He fingered the key ring in his pocket. How many Williams had held those keys? Too many. He pushed the door open and walked in.

No William blathered on and followed him down the hallway to one of the doors. He didn't miss the wheezing or heavy footfalls that would continually lag further and further behind.

Jack went to each door, peering in until he found one with a light on. "Hello?"

A young woman ran to the door. "What's going on? Why is everyone coming and going? Are we under attack?"

"No. I've come to let you out. The Williams are no longer in charge."

She cocked her head. "You sound like that stupid Simple. You're not working with him are you?"

"No. He's gone."

"He took some of my friends with him. I heard them go. What were they thinking, following an idiot like that?"

Jack made a note to keep this one away from the Simples. She wouldn't make his job any easier.

"You'll have first pick of the other Jacks." He certainly didn't want her for himself. "We have our own houses now, and you can live up there with us."

Her brown eyes grew round. "Can I live with you?"

Jack avoided her gaze by shuffling through the keys. "We'll have to see." He found one that unlocked the door. The girl watched the door open with her hands clasped under her chin and a giddy smile.

"Come on, help me find the others."

"They're probably all down in the bottom of the vault." She grabbed his hand. "I'll show you."

Jack let her lead him downward. The sloping, turning hallway finally opened into a large room that tugged at long-buried memories. A crowd of women and children stood behind a long wall broken by two wide doors bound together with a chain.

A smear of dried blood on the floor caught his eye. A trail led up the hallway. He looked from the blood to the doors.

An old woman regarded him with a scowl. "What the hell is going on? I demand to talk to a William right now. This breach has gone beyond reason. I will not stand for it a moment longer."

"Breach?" Jack cocked his head. "I'm here to set you all free." He reached for the lock, only to find there wasn't even one to open. A single tug pulled the chains from the handles.

"Get away from the door." The old woman swatted at his hands. "Why do you Jacks all assume we want to be free?"

"All?"

The old woman turned toward the others. "Muriel, give me your knife."

No one came forward.

"Matron, what happened here?" asked the young woman he'd freed.

"We defended ourselves from that damned Jack. Why are you out of your room, Willa?

Jack froze. "You killed Three? I thought it was the Williams, but it was you?" His mind spun.

"He invaded our space. Broke the rules. That Simple should have gotten the same treatment," said the Matron.

Jack's muscles quivered as adrenaline surged

through his body. He wasn't a William; he wouldn't slap her. He gripped the bars of the door instead. "I have overthrown the men who buried your babies in the garden and fed you from their rotting bodies, who took your children from you, who locked you in rooms for your entire lives. They may have fed you and kept everyone at a distance, but did you take men willingly into your bed? I don't think so. That makes you slaves."

She glared at him. "We do our duty. That is our will."

"You all agree with this?" he asked the women milling behind the Matron.

Slight shakes of their heads and downward stares answered his question as well as words.

"That's what I thought. Now, who gave you knives?"

"The Williams, silly," said Willa, draping her hand over his arm. "All the breeders have them in case the Wildmen ever make it down here."

"I've never seen these knives, and I've undressed my fair share of breeders."

Willa shrugged. "We have no reason to use them on Jacks." She glared at the other women inside. "Usually."

They had the good sense to continue gazing at the floor. He was half-inclined to find out who had hurt Three, but it seemed the old woman was the instigator.

Another woman came to the door, younger and less angry, with a child on her hip. "Did you see the others? The ones that left? Are they okay?"

"They were fine last I saw, headed into the Wildlands with the Simple."

"Joshua. His name was Joshua," said the woman.

"Yes, I know." He needed to remember names now and use them. It wasn't going to be an easy change to make.

"My sister was with them."

"One of them was shot, but she should be okay, it was barely a graze."

"You're sure she was okay?"

"I'm sure the other women will take care of her."

"We should have gone with them," she said under her breath as she headed back to the others.

Jack glanced at the blood on the floor again, wishing Three had lived to see the Williams overthrown. He sighed and pushed the doors open.

"The Williams are no longer in control. Stay down here if you wish or find a home with a suitable mate, be it a Jack or a Simple. Your children will no longer be taken from you. We will all work together to maintain the fortress and its safety."

The Matron's fingers tunneled into her thin white hair, raking her scalp. "You idiots! Our children are fed and cared for down here and so are we."

"By Williams," said Jack. "The Williams no longer serve you. They will teach your children. All of them. And yourselves if you so wish. You will be expected to work for your meals like the rest of us."

"But—" The Matron's pale, wrinkled face grew a shade whiter. "The only Isaiahs we have are mere children. They won't be helpful to our society for years. They have so much to learn. We need the Williams to teach them."

"Why? They are just children. Like all the others. I've seen the breeding book. Whatever work the men who began the program began has become pointless with so few of us left. If a Simple can rise up and compel half of you to join him on a quest to live outside these walls with nothing more than a ring of stolen keys and words, they're not as simple as we've been taught to believe. They'll make as good of mates as any."

"We'll need the equipment," she looked around wildly as if doing an inventory of things he couldn't see. "The farthest we can go is the decontamination chamber. There are rooms up there we can use, closer to the door. If you must entertain this notion of freedom, at least use sense."

Jack laughed. "That chamber hasn't worked in my lifetime, and probably most of yours. It was stripped a long time ago."

Her shriveled lips hung agape. "But...Isaiah would have told me if that were true."

"Apparently not." He shrugged. "We haven't had enough power for your precious equipment for years. If we can turn out the lights here, we can use what little power we have elsewhere."

"No," the Matron whispered as she stumbled backward until she reached a chair, which she dropped into as if she'd lost all the bones in her legs and spine. "Everything is lost. Lost. Pointless, all of it. We're ruined."

Jack turned to Willa. "Gather them up and lead them up the ramp. We'll work on finding sleeping arrangements for those of you who don't already have a mate in mind. Be sure to bring everything of use with you, blankets and such, we don't have such nice things up top."

Willa rushed into the room and started herding children toward their mothers.

"And if I catch any of you using a knife on anyone up top, you'll be moving into the jail. We don't hurt our own around here."

Thinking of hurting people, gave him an idea, one that would take care of two problems at once.

"You know what? I have just the place for you, Matron. You can tell the Williams just what you think of them and their lies." He picked up the old woman and tossed her over his shoulder.

She hung there, limp, muttering how freedom would be the end of them all.

The others followed, blankets and children in hand as they made their way upward. Along the way, he used keys to release a young woman with a plain face and short straw-colored hair from one of the rooms. Assured by Willa that all the remaining women were accounted for, he led them out of the artificial light and into the gazes of a hundred pairs of eager eyes.

Jack made a note to have a talk with Two as he

placed himself as a barricade between the men and the women.

"The women choose. Everyone else, keep your hands to yourselves or you'll find yourself sitting beside a William." He kept his gaze on the men before him while speaking over his shoulder. "If you know the mate you'd like, go to him now. Otherwise, stay behind me and we'll find a safe place for you until you're ready to choose."

"Why do we have to choose?" asked one of the breeders with a little girl in her arms. "Maybe I don't want a mate."

"Muriel," chided Willa, "you're just upset about your Jack. There are plenty more. But not this one." Willa wrapped her arms around him from behind, pressing her breasts against the thin shirt that covered his back.

As much as he didn't mind that sensation, dealing with her hateful attitude of the Simples wasn't something he had time for. He pried her off and grabbed the hand of the brown-eyed girl he'd freed from the last room.

"Sorry, this one already spoke for me. Didn't you?"

"He's toying with you, Georgia," hissed the Matron from his shoulder.

He squeezed the old woman tight, hoping to push all the air from her spiteful lungs. She coughed twice and then went silent.

Georgia's brows crinkled together and she glanced from Jack to Willa and back again. She licked her lips and started to shake her head.

"Don't worry about her," Jack said. "She won't hold a grudge. We're all friends here, right?" He gave her hand a squeeze.

"Right. Yes," she said uncertainly.

Willa scowled, looking at their hands. "Oh fine. I claim the young one then. He's cuter anyway." She ran to Two's side.

Two of the other women went to Jacks, their children in tow. The rest remained behind him.

"You'll have to give them time. Now get to work. All of you have jobs to do." He waved the men off with his free hand.

Two by three the men wandered off until they were alone. He quickly made for the jail and deposited the Matron in the cell where Three had died. She could enjoy the smell of the death she'd caused until he decided what to do with her for the long term.

The Williams eyed him in silence. They were learning quickly.

Jack left the jail with the crowd of women and children, walking as fast as they could keep up with. "I'll put you in the house we used for now. The Simples were promised this building, so I'd recommend making other arrangements soon. I'd also recommend barring the door at night until the Simples get used to this arrangement. They've not seen a woman since childhood and most of them have never entertained the idea of being with one as the Williams rarely allowed it. Let me know immediately if there are any problems."

He held the door open to the old Jack house. "I'll give you until morning to get settled. You'll get your work assignments at breakfast."

With the women safely secured, he brought Georgia to his house. "It's small, but it's ours."

She stepped inside and spun around to face him. "Are you sure you'd rather have me than Willa? I've not had a baby yet. She's had two. I don't even know if I can."

Jack sat down on the bed. "I didn't want Willa. We'll deal with the rest."

She sat down beside him. "And what about the Wildmen? What if they come back and we're up here where they can get us?"

"They have women now. The ones Joshua left with. If anything, they'll be after food. Food, I'm willing to trade for, but not people."

She offered him a shy smile. "I don't care what the Matron said, I like you better than the Williams already."

CHAPTER FIFTEEN

Joshua watched Grace and two young boys pick peaches from a tree they'd found behind the remnants of the building beside the library. Three of the juicy treasures rested in the bag that hung from a long strap over his right shoulder along with a hard crust of bread and a plastic container heavy with water. He'd eaten more since they'd reached the library than he had in the week before. He didn't mind being a little hungry if that meant knowing that Susan and the others had plenty of food in case he couldn't come back right away. Or at all. He swallowed hard.

"I'm coming with you," announced Emelda.

"And them?" He pointed at her two children.

"In case I have to stay there, I want my children with me." She held out her hand to one of the Simples. "This is Emma. She doesn't have any children of her own yet, but she'd like to. Isn't that right, Emma?"

Emma nodded, wrapping her green sweater around herself like a giant hug. "I like babies," she said, watching Joshua out of the corners of her eyes.

"You both have food?"

"Oh yes," Emelda said, holding up a bag like his. "Susan made sure we were well stocked. We also have a map from one of the books. We have a good guess as to where the Wildmen are."

Having a map and someone to read it made him feel much better.

Emma pointed to the bag at her feet. "We have lots of tasty treats."

Joshua spotted Susan in the crowd. She ran her hands through her son's hair, smoothing the mop of curls. Far away in his memory, he remembered the soothing touch of his mother's fingers as she'd done the same for him. He ran a hand through over his hair, the tangled mess on his head catching on his ragged fingernails.

He sighed and turned to Emelda. "They might keep you."

"We know. It's all right, Joshua. Thank you for being so concerned." Emelda leaned in close. "You might want to talk to Susan before we go."

He wasn't sure what to say, but he picked his way over to her. "I guess we're leaving."

Susan shooed her children off and stood. "Then take this." She held out her knife in a worn brown sheath. Two pairs of lacings hung from it. "Go ahead, put it on. You have a belt. That will make it easier than trying to hide it under a skirt."

"You should keep it. You need to protect them." He motioned to the women and children surrounding them.

"Do you know how to use a knife?" she asked.

"Yes. William-four told us how."

"Then you take it. I'm sure we can find more weapons here if we need to."

She knelt down and untied his belt, slipping the rope through the top loop. Then she reached around his thigh tying the second lacing there. His pants were suddenly very tight. Joshua stared at the brown stains on the ceiling while she took what seemed like forever adjusting the lacing. She stood and smiled at him. "There. You'll keep them safe, won't you?"

"Yes."

"Good. I'll miss you, Joshua."

"I'll miss you too. Make sure you stay inside at night. Don't let the children wander off. And keep everyone fed and warm." His mouth kept talking even though his fluttering stomach wanted him to stop.

"I will." She pressed her finger to his lips. "I'll be waiting for you, so you better come back, okay?"

He gulped and nodded.

"Good." She kissed him. Not just a peck on the cheek, but really kissed him.

Joshua's stomach leapt into his throat, and for a moment, he forgot to breathe.

Susan broke away and stepped back.

Joshua grinned. "I'm going to go now so I can come back very soon."

"You do that." She gave him a gentle push toward the door where Emelda and Emma waited.

Outside the library, they passed rows of

crumbling houses and the place where they'd found the berries. They passed where the stream ran near the path and walked until Emelda's children could no longer keep up. She carried one and he carried the other for while. The soft hair of the boy in his arms tickled his chin as a breeze picked up. The wind rushed over them, bringing goosebumps to his skin. Only Emma, with her sweater, didn't seem to mind the chill. They stopped for a quick bite to eat and a few swallows of water before continuing on. Emelda wrapped her blanket around herself and the boy she carried.

The apples hadn't even started to turn red yet at the fortress. They should have three or four months yet before the snow started to fall, he assured himself. It was just a cold wind. They would have time to stock food away for winter. At least they didn't have winters like the ones Williams told of from faraway places, where snow fell to men's waists and higher. They could still hunt. If he could get a gun, or the Wildmen could teach him how to trap small animals or get fish from the stream.

Joshua looked down at the chubby boy in his arms, almost old enough to be removed from the vault. Red splotches stained his cheeks. His very own William.

Emma came up to walk beside him. "His name is Michael. He's going to be a William. I hope he will be a good William."

"He won't." He never wanted to hear that name again.

"No?" Emma's steps slowed. "That's too bad. He's a good boy."

"Then he will be a good Michael."

"Oh good." Emma smiled, revealing widely spaced teeth. Then she seemed to forget he was there at all as she clapped her hands and hummed quietly just behind him.

"This way," Emelda said, pointing from the setting sun. "North and East."

They traveled for days, walking and resting, taking turns carrying the two boys, sleeping inside old buildings when they came across them. Joshua found grapevines and berries along the way and a handful of mushrooms that Jacks had told him were safe to eat. Rain had fallen on them twice and his legs were very tired of walking.

As the sun sunk low on the horizon on the fifth day, a man who looked like a strip of dried meat stopped them. The children, tired and dirty, clung to Emelda. She and Emma stood close behind Joshua. Joshua smiled at the dark-skinned man and said, "Hello."

"Hello yourself." He eyed the women, looking them up and down. A grin revealed yellow and brown teeth.

"Are you one of the Wildmen?"

"I might be. Who are you?"

"I'm Joshua. Phillip was my friend. Do you know Phillip?"

The skinny man scowled. "That old nut died in the last attack on the damned fortress."

"No, he was captured," Joshua told the man about freeing Phillip and how he'd brought these two women with him just like Phillip had wanted. It wasn't all the truth, but he didn't want to tell them about Susan or the others and so he told himself it was okay to lie a little this once.

He pulled the coin from his pocket and showed it to the Wildman. "Phillip gave me this."

"That's his, all right." He sucked in his cheeks, making him look even more dried up. "Can't believe the old man did it. You can leave the women with me."

"We're all tired and they don't know if they want to stay with you."

Now that he was here and talking to the Wildman, he wasn't sure this was a good idea. His insides felt all squirmy.

This man wasn't Phillip. Phillip had been like a William and Jack put together, but he didn't know this man at all.

"I suppose we can let you all stay the night since you did bring us such a generous gift."

He didn't feel much like he was giving the man a gift. It didn't make him feel warm and good inside like when he'd given Susan the necklace. Seeing the Wildman look at Emelda like he did made Joshua mad. "Don't look at her like that. It's not nice, and they're not a gift."

"All right then. No need to get mad about it. You can call me Harold. Come on, we'll see what old Tom has to say about the lot of you."

The tumbled remains of buildings lay scattered across the ground like a giant wind had picked them up and thrown them around. Here and there wood and metal stood propped against big squares of gray stone to form what looked like patched-together buildings that had also fallen to ruin. Hollow-eyed people crept out from behind the stones to watch them walk by. Boys, boney and tanned from the sun, pointed at them and whispered.

A gray-haired man emerged from a brick-lined hole in the ground. As they got closer, Joshua noticed cement steps leading downward.

"Wait here." Harold went to speak to the old man. He nodded at Joshua and the women now and then. Both of them pointed at Emelda's children.

"I'm Tom," said the old man as the two walked over to them. "You're called Joshua?"

He nodded. "We came from the fortress."

"So I heard. Didn't know there were any Joshua's in the fortress."

"We're new."

Tom scowled. "You look like a Simple to me. A big one, but still a Simple, and better fed than any one of us. You bring us some food along with these women?"

More men came up from the hole, dirty and skinny and looking at him with sunken eyes. They gathered behind Tom and Harold.

Joshua tapped the knife on his leg, wondering if he should draw it or not. There were so many Wildmen all around him, but when he looked closer, he noticed almost all of them were young boys. Most were past the age where they'd have lived outside the vault and a few were almost adults. Only a handful of the crowd were as old as Harold, and Tom was the only gray-hair. Joshua wasn't afraid of children.

"Well?"

"No, we ran out of food two days ago." Joshua patted the knife again and thought of Susan. "How many people do you have here?"

"Enough."

Two women shambled up the stairs. One walked with a crutch as she was missing her leg from the knee down. The face of the other one was caved in on one side, her eye seeming to have slid down to rest atop her cheek. They wore rags, far worse than anything even the lowest Simple had in the fortress.

"Is that all? Two women?" asked Joshua.

"Last two winters brought a sickness that killed the rest, but we've got four now," said Tom. He nodded to the other grown men.

Joshua drew his knife and made sure Emelda and Emma were right behind him. Emelda had her knife out too and Emma held hands with both of the boys. "Phillip said you lost many of your Simples in the attack?"

"Our poor men, yes, we did." Tom and the others stared at his knife and halted their approach. "We lost a lot of people in that attack, but we needed to get inside."

"Why?"

"Why? Because you have everything and we

have nothing! Because your Williams burned our fathers alive. Because they turned on us, called us filth and rats. They used to trade, didn't begrudge us a bit of sharing from their fields, but then they got greedy. Our treasures weren't good enough for them anymore. They killed our strong men, and took their fields inside their walls and left us here to starve. We're dying here."

"Why didn't you go somewhere else?" asked Joshua.

Tom gave him the same look as Williams did when they were about to hit him upside the head. "Because everything we need is right inside those damned walls. All we have to do is get to it. It's right there, so close we can smell the pigs and cows when the wind is right."

"There are other places."

"There are. We've tried them. Sent men out, but they don't come back. Maybe they just leave. Maybe they die. We don't know cause they don't tell us. But your kind," He tsked. "Bet you didn't know we've got some of you over the years. William's will tell you a bear gets those who don't report back, but some just leave. Like you." He winked. "They come looking for a new home. They bring news from the fortress."

"Do you have news for us, Joshua?" asked Harold

"Phillip told us you would give us a home here."

"What we want is to know how to get in there," Tom said. "You tell me that, and I might let you stay with the women."

Joshua turned to Emelda. She shook her head. Her friends were still at the fortress. His friends too. And the other Jacks.

"No. There are other places to live. You don't need the fortress."

"Places with electricity? With livestock and gardens?" He shook his head. "We've looked."

"There could be. You don't need the other things. Don't you know how to plant your own fields?"

"Rats ate our seed stores years ago. Where are we supposed to get more? The Williams won't trade for them. They don't care about us." Tom's face turned red. "The only animals we've got are rats. Grow them all year, harvest any time you like, and they find their own food—mostly among their own dead and ours—never a shortage there. Bears make good eating too if you don't lose too many men taking one down. But do you see many men around here? Do you? The Jacks and Williams killed them all. Selfish bastards."

"I could show you how to make gardens." But there would be no babies or Williams in his garden. Not ever. "Can you show us how to be safe from bears?"

"What, are we trading now? How do we know you won't run back to the Jacks and tell them where to find us so they can wipe us out once and for all?"

Emelda stepped up next to Joshua. "We've left the fortress. We're not going back there."

Tom shook his head. "You had everything there."

"We had too many Williams there," said Joshua. "Bad Williams. The Jacks will take care of them now."

"Well now, a change of the guard, huh?" Tom licked his chapped lips. "Could mean the fortress is less defended. We should attack."

Harold shook his head. "Attack with what, our children? If the Jacks will shoot the poor men down, you can bet they'll shoot the kids. Are you ready to send your sons to their deaths?"

"They're not all my sons," said Tom as he surveyed the surrounding children.

The other men scowled at Tom, their hands forming fists at their sides.

Emelda leaned in close and whispered, "Invite them, Joshua. They've got nothing here. We could use more men. They could use more women."

Joshua bit his lip. If there were more men, Susan might not be so nice to him anymore.

"Joshua," Emelda hissed in his ear.

If it meant that he wouldn't have to leave Emma and Emelda with these men, then maybe getting her friend back would make Susan happy enough to keep being nice to him even if there were other men to pick from. "We have a place to live with a roof and walls and food. You could live there too."

"What place? Where?" asked Tom.

Emelda said, "Five days west from here."

The old man scowled. "That's even farther from

the fortress."

"You don't need the fortress," said Emelda.

"Why don't you come down and spend the night with us while we discuss it?"

"We'll stay up here, thank you," she said.

"Suit yourself. We have a nice stew cooking down there if you get hungry," said Tom.

"We'll be fine. Give us your answer in the morning, and we'll be on our way." Emelda tugged Joshua backward several steps. She pointed at a tumble of bricks and metal rods. "That looks like a good place to spend the night."

It didn't to Joshua, but Emelda seemed intent on doing what she wanted, so he went along with her. Emma followed with Emelda's children.

Tom, Harold, and the others filed down the stairs. A few older boys lingered nearby, talking quietly amongst themselves, but they too eventually wandered down the hole.

Hungry, cold and without a roof over his head, Joshua laid down with his blanket. Emelda's children settled in behind him, their bodies offering a little warmth.

"Sleep, Joshua," Emelda said. "I'll watch over us for a little while."

He did sleep, but when she called his name, he woke in an instant.

"Someone's out there," she whispered. "Emma, wake up."

"How about you just let her sleep and take off?" suggested a voice from the darkness. "We'll be good to her, don't you worry."

Someone else snickered. "Oh yeah, we'll treat her just fine. Live like a queen here, she will."

"Queen of rats," said another.

"Go on. We'll say your good-bye's for you."

"No," said Joshua.

This wasn't at all what Phillip had talked about. These Wildmen weren't happy to see him. They weren't nice, and they certainly didn't have food. Phillip had lied to the women and to him. He grabbed the coin from his pocket and threw it at the voices as hard as he could.

"Ow. He hit me. How did he do that in the dark?"

"Joshua can see in the dark, and next time he's throwing a knife. You better run," said Emelda.

Footsteps scampered away until he was left with nothing but the chirping of crickets and the pounding of his own heart.

"They were young," said Emelda. "Lucky it wasn't the older men. They wouldn't have left so easily."

"I can't see in the dark," said Joshua.

"I know."

"I can't either," said Emma.

"None of us can. Joshua, would you mind taking watch for a while. I need to rest."

"Sure." He was too awake to sleep now anyway.

The women curled under the blankets behind him and Joshua stared out into the darkness, wishing he could, in fact, see in the dark. Every little noise made him jump and he was sure he heard footsteps, but they stayed at a distance. He kept his knife in his hand just in case.

When the first hint of sunlight crept over the horizon, he did see movement. A man. Two men. Heading toward them. Joshua stood up, pulled out his knife and called out to Emelda. Emma woke too and pulled the boys close, telling them to stay quiet.

Emelda and Joshua, with knives in hand, met Harold and another of the Wildmen.

"Awake already?" said Harold.

"Come with your answer so early?" asked Emelda.

Harold glanced at the other man, who nodded. "Old Tom is intent on staying here. The rest of us aren't so sure. Either way, we lost too many of our hunters in that last attack. We've got too many mouths to feed."

"So if we would stay here with you, we would starve," said Emelda.

"No, we'd feed you. Not your kids though. Don't need more of them running around. We need girl children. Your Simple would have to hunt for you and himself. And the rest of us. Got to feed the women first. We get what's left, and if there are scraps, they go to our kids. Outsiders last."

Joshua gripped his knife tight. "Even if I gather food, I don't get to eat?"

"Don't work that way here."

"Then I don't want to be here," he declared. "We're leaving."

Emelda nodded. She motioned to Emma, who stood with the boys in her arms. They all stepped out of the shelter and started to back away.

"Wait," said Harold. "You said you have a place."

Joshua nodded, taking another step backward.

"If we can't talk Tom out of it, he'll take another stab at the fortress. He's sure that, with the Williams gone, he can hit hard before the Jacks get settled in. He'll throw our sons at the walls and they'll die. Like our men always do."

"Maybe you should have a change of the guard too," said Emelda.

Harold nodded. "Some of us have considered that very thing. But not everyone agrees. So here's the deal. You stay," he said, pointing to Emelda. "That one can take the kids with Joshua and get out of here before Tom and his men come up here and take both of you by force. They'll kill Joshua and the boys."

Emma started crying. Emelda gasped.

Joshua's hands shook, the grip of the knife digging into his skin. "They would kill me? They would kill the boys we worked so hard to bring here?"

He imagined stabbing them. Stabbing all of them, until his face was covered in red splatters like the women's had been when they'd killed the William in the vault. His teeth hurt and his jaw ached, and he felt like every little muscle along his back and neck stood out like an angry dog with his fur standing up.

Harold stepped back, bumping into the other man behind him. He held out his empty hands. "Now. Now. No need to get all riled up. We can work something out. Something that we both agree on."

His heart pounded in his ears. He tried very hard to make the bloody pictures in his head stop. "We need boys. Older boys. Boys who can hunt and catch fish and fight animals. We will feed them."

"And what do you propose to trade for these boys?" asked Harold.

He couldn't leave Emelda here, not if these men would hurt her boys. The other men hadn't sounded like they would take good care of Emma either. Emma needed help sometimes, like many of his friends. She would be scared here all alone.

"Emma will stay," declared Emelda. "But only if you promise she's looked after. She's a sweet girl and nothing would make her happier than to have babies of her own."

"Stay here?" asked Emma. "Just me?"

"You'll be fine, dear," said Emelda.

Harold looked to the man behind him. "She's better off than what we've got left."

"Tom's not going to like it."

"Tom doesn't like much. We need a new woman around here."

"Emma for ten boys," said Joshua, watching the hole in the distance for any sign of Tom.

Harold rubbed his chin. "Tell you what, I'll send along my oldest. I'll not let old Tom kill him in one last try at those walls. What do you think?"

"Could be sending him off to his death with these two," said the other man.

"At least he'll be going off to death beside a pretty woman. Better ending than I'll ever get."

The other man clapped Harold's shoulder. "So true.

"All right then, you'll get your ten," said Harold.

"You don't have to end here," said Emelda. "We have plenty of room. Tom can't attack the fortress if he doesn't have men to do it for him."

"She's got a point, Harold."

"We'll think about it."

"All I ask then, is if you do leave," said Emelda, "you bring Emma with you."

The hope that Emma might come back to them made his shoulders feel a little lighter. Susan would like that too.

Emelda pulled out her map and looked it over. "If you choose to join us, wait here." She pointed to the spot they'd stayed on the second night. "We will send someone to look now and then. There's shelter there. You'll be safe for awhile."

Harold nodded. "We'll send the boys up and then you leave us the girl."

"Her name is Emma," said Joshua.

"Right. Then Emma will be staying with us."

Emma looked uncertainly at Emelda and the boys who sat beside her. "I don't want to stay by myself."

Joshua watched as the two men jogged back to

the hole. One went down. The other stayed at the edge, keeping an eye on them. There wasn't enough light yet to see which was which. He sat beside Emma and put his arm around her. "There are lots of children here, and they need your help. You know how to be nice to them. Teach them to be nice too."

Emma sniffed and nodded a little.

"We will see you again soon, I think," said Emelda. She hugged her boys to her, ruffling their hair and kissing their cheeks.

The golden edge of the sun had just peeked over the horizon when the first boy emerged from the hole and made his way toward them. A moment later, two more followed. Then another and another. They moved fast and quiet. It wasn't until the first boy reached him that Joshua noticed Harold and five more boys were also coming their way.

Emelda let her boys go and hugged Emma. When she let her go, Emma fisted her sweater in a white-knuckled grip but didn't cry.

The first boy was almost grown, with big shoulders and long legs. "Isaac," he said, thumping his chest and looking him right in the eye.

That made him uncomfortable, itchy all over, but he didn't look away. He waited for the boy to say something else or look somewhere else. Isaac didn't.

The other boys gathered up around them, and then Harold was there too. Joshua could see him out of the corner of his eye.

"Boy, I told you to listen to Joshua. You want a full belly, you better behave. I hear different, you'll answer for it."

"Yes, Pa." Isaac dropped his gaze to the ground and backed away a couple steps.

"Come on then," he held out his hand toward Emma. "We best all be on our way before old Tom stirs."

Emma gave Joshua one last glance before going to Harold's side. She didn't hold his hand, but she did follow as he led her to the hole.

"Joshua, we need to go," said Emelda.

The boys, ranging from a little older than Emelda's sons to not quite as old as Isaac, bunched around them as they walked. They glanced over their shoulders now and then but didn't say a word.

Joshua tried to remember what the Williams did with new Simples fresh from the vault. Those little boys were sad too and they missed their mothers and the vault. They were scared in a big new place with all new people. Williams yelled at the little boys and told them to stop crying and to be brave and do their jobs.

He didn't want to yell. He decided to pass the time walking back the way they'd come by asking each boy their name and what jobs they knew how to do.

All of them knew how to find food, and they proved it along the way by catching frogs. They showed him their knives. He showed them his, making sure to not let it go so they couldn't take it or let it get too far from his hand when he did put it away in case he needed it. He shouldn't have agreed to take so many boys. There were too many to keep an eye on. Too many of them and not enough of he and Emelda. She kept her own boys close to her.

By the time they stopped for the night, he was so tired, but he didn't dare sleep. He needed to keep Emelda safe. They could kill him and take her back to their home. They'd kill her boys. Harold had said so.

He watched the boys make a fire and cook the frogs. They ate them, offering some of the meat to Emelda.

"Everyone eats," he said, getting to his feet. He grabbed half of the meat from the nearest boys hand and divided it between Emelda's boys. Then he looked to Isaac. He held out his hand, keeping his other on the knife on his leg.

Isaac stood and stared at him again, flames reflecting on his eyes. There was no Harold to help him now. He had to be like Jack, telling the boys what to do. "I said, everyone," he said louder this time.

His hand didn't move and neither did his eyes. The flames danced. The other boys shifted around, watching Isaac.

Isaac faded, becoming a William telling him he couldn't eat, that there wasn't enough food for him. He became a coat-clad William standing at the fortress door, telling him to run the paths again even though his fingers were numb and his teeth wouldn't stop chattering. He was William-fourteen telling him that he was going to be killed and that no one would miss him.

Susan would miss him. And he wasn't going to let anyone keep him from getting back to the library, to her. He struck Isaac, knocking him sideways. The boy staggered, tripping over the others who sat around him. He fell face first into the dirt.

One of the other boys grabbed the food from Isaac's hand and held it out. "This is yours."

Joshua grabbed it and took a bite of the juicy meat, savoring it. He took another before he started to feel bad for the boy lying on the ground. Handing what was left of the meat to Emelda, he grabbed Isaac's hand and pulled him to his feet.

"Here." He wiped the worst of the dirt from the boy's face. "Now sit down and eat." Joshua handed the meat back to Isaac.

That's when he noticed what he'd thought was just dirt hadn't wiped off. It was a bruise. On his forehead.

"Where were you last night?" Joshua asked.

Isaac rubbed his jaw where Joshua had hit him, keeping his gaze on his lap.

Joshua looked to Emelda. She nodded.

"Remember, I can see in the dark," Joshua said. He turned to the whole group of boys. "Put your knives and any other weapons you have in my bag. You'll get them back when it's time to hunt for food tomorrow."

The boys tossed their knives onto the ground at his feet. Isaac set his on top of the pile.

"Thank you." Joshua put the knives away and sat

next to Emelda.

Once all the boys had finished their dinner and were on the ground quiet. Emelda leaned close and whispered, "Well done, Joshua. Susan will be very proud of you."

With the bag of weapons clutched to his chest, Joshua passed the night with dreams of Susan, of Emma alone with the Wildmen, and of fire twisting and turning in Isaac's eyes.

He woke feeling as though he hadn't slept at all. Darkness hung below Emelda's eyes. The boys appeared well rested, chatting quietly amongst themselves. Isaac kept to himself as they started off.

One of the younger boys walked beside Joshua for a little while before he began to talk about how to make a spear from a stick and how to tie a knife to it and how his father had killed a bear with that very thing once. He talked about his father, his brothers and the bearskin they slept under. He talked so much that Joshua longed for it to be night again. At least then the boys were silent.

Two of the older boys offered to carry Emelda's children on their shoulders for a while and one offered to carry her bag. All of them smiled at her, even Isaac.

As they passed the days walking, Joshua told the boys of the clothes they'd found, how sweet the peaches were and about the clean water that flowed through the stream. Emelda sang songs, bits of which he remembered from his childhood.

The boys took turns walking beside him or

Emelda, carrying her bag, walking with or carrying her sons. As the trickle of the stream near the path cut through his thoughts, Joshua noticed it was Isaac who walked beside him.

"I bet my father was here once. They don't let us go very far anymore, now that there are so few of us left, but here I am." He grinned. "This is way nicer than home."

"We're not there yet," Joshua said as he led them all down the path to the big brick building.

He heard the high pitched shouts before he saw the women. They spilled down the stairs and ran to meet them. Madeline and Susan stood at the top of the steps with their knives in hand. Joshua waved to them as he'd seen the Jack do to his fellow Jacks on the walls. Susan put her knife away and came to him. She wrapped her arms around his waist and kissed him.

Joshua kissed her back, not minding the jumping in his stomach or the racing of his heart one tiny bit. They stayed that way for a long moment before he remembered all the other people with him.

He cleared his throat until he found the voice from deep inside him again. "They're here to join us."

Susan squeezed his hand. "That's wonderful news. Where's Emma?"

"We had to trade with Harold. Tom didn't like us. He wanted to attack the fortress. But Emma may come back if Harold can get others to come live here. They have nothing there. It was a sad place," he said.

"Then let's hope Harold is successful. We'll need more room if they do." She surveyed the surrounding buildings. "It would keep those new boys busy to start fixing one of the other houses."

Madeline came forward and took charge of the newcomers. The boys looked after Emelda with longing faces, especially the older ones.

Susan giggled. "Well, we know who to put in charge of them."

Somewhere in the crowd, Isaac laughed. Joshua spotted the tall boy talking to two of the older girls. He didn't look at them like his father had looked at Emma and Emelda. That made Joshua happy.

"Come inside the library. I want to show you something," Susan tugged on his hand. "My mother had a favorite book that she often read to me when I was little. When she died I looked for it, but I couldn't find it. The Williams probably took it for themselves."

She brought him to a stand where a thick book with gold-edged pages lay open.

"When I first saw you in the vault and heard you speak of leaving the fortress, it reminded me of something she'd read to me. I found that book here and spent an entire day reading to find the right words." She rested her fingertips on the page and ran them under the words as she read.

Joshua found himself unable to concentrate on what she said. He watched her lips move, the way her hair fell against her face as she leaned over the book.

Then she looked up and caught his gaze and smiled. He closed his eyes so he could pay attention.

"It says here: But the meek shall inherit the earth; and shall delight themselves in the abundance of peace. Who are we if not the meek?"

He thought of the William in the garden and the tiny babies he'd found there. He thought of Arianne alone against her cold wall. Of Jack in his cell, and Phillip laying under the open sky, of the Jacks who walked the walls and all the women left in the vault who chose to stay behind. Joshua wished them all an abundance of peace.

He squeezed Susan's hand and she cast him a sideways grin. Amidst the delighted squeals of children playing, they headed outside.

EPILOGUE

Lucas approached the pale form on his father's bed, his sweating palms held firmly at his sides. He hoped his mother didn't notice. "Papa?"

"I'm okay, Lucas, don't be scared." The big man struggled to set up and settled for bunching the pillows behind his head. "They tell me I'll be fine." He smiled the same smile that had always warmed Lucas inside.

His father might be odd, some called him slow, the ones at the fortress whispered the word *Simple*, but no one dared say those things to his face. Joshua was a *legend*, that's what the others called him, the stragglers they traded with. That word he didn't mind, though he would shake his head and tell them that wasn't true. But Lucas had grown up hearing stories from the others who had followed his father from the life they'd known, both those who had lived in the fortress and the ones who had once been known as Wildmen. It was hard having a legend for a father.

And his father had been ill for weeks. Now the trading time was upon them and his shoulders stiffened with what he knew his father was about to ask.

"You know I can't go to watch over the trades. Your mother won't let me. I need you to go for me, Lucas." He held out his hand.

Lucas crept closer and took it, his own fingers engulfed in the giant hand. No matter that he was sixteen and near full grown himself, his father had always been a big man. He always would be, Lucas assured himself. Men like his father couldn't die from getting sick. Most of his hair wasn't even all grey yet.

He glanced at his mother. The lines on her face grew deeper every day and white strands sparkled among the dark on her head. She gave him a reassuring smile.

He'd done his best to help her since his father had fallen ill, watching over his three sisters and working with the others to keep the town running as Joshua would have. But he wasn't his father. He was thin like his mother. No matter how much he ate, his shoulders didn't widen to fill the doorway like his father's. He might be strong, but his body didn't show it. And now he was going to have to go to the trade and watch over the giant men who managed the fortress, men like his father, but they could be cunning, and their smiles, on lips much like the ones he knew, didn't make him warm inside. They were hard men.

The clammy grasp of his father's hand reminded him that he should answer. "I'll go."

"Don't worry," his mother said, joining them by

the bedside. "I'll keep order here while you're gone."

Lucas had no doubt of that. The people of the town might think that his father was in charge, but behind closed doors, it was his mother that put the wise words in the mouth of the man who was built to enforce them. She'd been working with Isaac and a few of the other men for the past couple weeks. They would have to do in his absence.

His father let go of him to cover his mouth for a round of hacking coughs. Tears ran down his face and the muscles in his neck stood out. The entire bed shook. When his throat was clear again, he said, "Don't let those Jack's take advantage of anyone."

"I won't." He'd been going with to trade since he could walk. He knew his father's role just fine. But his father wouldn't be there. He would. And he wasn't supposed to call them Jacks. Only his father could get away with that.

"Good. Ask after Emma and send along the treats your mother set aside for her children."

"I will."

He started to cough again. "Don't take your sisters. Your mother needs them here."

His mother's thinned lips and a pointed look at Lucas, let him know he'd reached her limit of patience. And very likely not just with him.

"I'll be going as soon as we load up the last of the supplies then. Be well, Papa."

His father started to try to say something else but the coughing took over again. "Joshua," his mother said. "Enough. Get some rest. You've trained

Lucas well. He'll handle it." She looked to Lucas. "And you take care of yourself."

He considered giving his mother a hug, but she was already bent over his father, holding him while he caught his breath. Maybe this year he'd find someone at the trade that would take care of him like his mother took care of his father.

It was time for him to move out on his own. He'd had his eye on place for the past year, but one thing after another had come up, a storm, searching for livestock in the wilds, building a new enclosure for the animals they found, helping with the farming, and then helping to build a home for a family of scavengers that had decided to settle down.

With every new person that joined their growing town, Lucas was a little more in awe of his father. He sat at the table with them, sharing the same meal, listening to the conversation as it unfolded—each time a little differently, no two people were the same—but he could never quite put his finger on the moment where his father would sell them on staying. He would ask plain questions, explain the rules, tell them what the town had to offer and what was expected of each tenant, and almost all of them said yes. The ones that didn't, never quite said no either. They just weren't ready to settle yet. And every now and then, they would show back up, sometimes months, sometimes years later, but they would, ready to join the town.

He knew his father wasn't like many of the other men, that he saw things differently, more plainly, but while his mother helped with more intricate plans, it was his father that drew people in. They trusted him. Like Lucas hoped they would trust him someday.

Lucas gathered up his sack of extra clothes and food for the road and left his parents in the home they'd built at the center of the town.

Two boys held the horses, feeding them apples while the last of the trade goods were loaded onto the long wagon. He surveyed the crowd, many of whom were also carrying travel sacks bulging with supplies. He might not be going with his father, but he certainly wasn't going alone.

Two small bodies plowed into him with giggles. One wrapped scrawny arms around his thighs, the other his waist.

Teresa waited until they'd let go before swooping in to half strangle him with her iron-grip hug. "You better be careful."

"I will. Take care of everyone while I'm gone."

She nodded solemnly then wavered into a grin. "Bring me back a cute boy. A smart one."

"I'll see what I can do." He poked her in the ribs and swung the pack over his shoulder.

Taking one look back at the house next to the library and the handful of others that marked the original settlers, he took hold of the rope and led the horses out of town. They passed the tenants working the gardens that were sprinkled about on both sides of the main street. The foundations of some of the ancient homes that had been harvested to build new ones now served as pens for the animals they found. The flock of sheep was nearly in need of a second pen. Chickens roamed free, scattering noisily as the wagon passed with its crowd of followers. Some were coming to look for possible mates, others to trade their own goods or visit with friends who either remained with the scavengers or lived in the fortress. Some had simply come, as they always did, to assist with the town's trade goods.

He glanced at the park the children had claimed, an expanse of green grass with trees overhead, the leaves just beginning to turn yellow. And there, next to it was the lot where he wanted to build his own place someday soon, pulling supplies from the ancient houses, and cutting new lumber from the trees at the edge of town.

He'd traveled this way so many times that he wasn't nervous. When he was little, before his father would take him along, the trade land was much farther away, days of travel.

But now, the town wasn't a secret. Travelers stopped in, traded and moved on throughout the year. The road was clearly a road, traveled with ruts and footsteps, not something one could hide any longer. Now the trade was done a day's walk from town, requiring the scavengers and the fortress dwellers to do the bulk of the traveling. Here, in the town, that's where the majority of the population lived, so the others now came to them.

They stopped along the way for a midday meal and to fill their water jugs at the stream that ran near the curve of the road. Then they continued on, reaching the field by evening.

The field wasn't much of a field anymore, it had been set up with lean-to shelters over the years, more and more were added as more people came. Those that had traveled for days stayed the night after the trade day. Occasionally the day turned into two when the deals were trickier, as was often the case of swapping potential mates between groups. This year, Lucas was fully ready to stay three days if needed. He just hoped a suitable girl would be there. Teresa might want a boy, but she was only fourteen. She could wait a couple years. He was more than ready to do his part for the community right now.

Several of the shelters were already occupied. Some were scavengers, but the fortress dwellers were already in attendance too, the hulking forms of three Jacks shadowed three of the shelters, with more average-sized people filling the rest.

One of the large forms rose and headed over toward him. He was the youngest of ones his father still called Jacks, the one who called himself Jack Sutton. Lucas never quite understood why the big men hadn't shed their assigned names, but his father just smiled and called them stubborn. He said it was part of what made them Jacks. Instead, they'd adopted surnames from the book that had once been sacred to the men who had ruled the fortress.

As it was proper, Lucas addressed him by his surname and not as his father would have. He made sure his hand was dry and held it out, praying his voice didn't waver. "Greetings, Sutton."

"Greetings, Lucas. How fares your father?"

"He is ill. A cold, he says." Though this cold seemed to linger far longer than any cold Lucas had seen and the coughing was painful to even watch.

"His illness worries you. You think it's not a cold?"

Lucas's shoulders slumped. He didn't want Sutton to think him weak. The fortress dwellers would take advantage of him. But Sutton had seen the truth. Nothing Lucas could do about that now.

"It's held on too long."

Sutton surprised him by patting his shoulder. "I'll send Ingrid along with you when we're done here. She's been studying the medicine book we got at the very first trade since she could read."

He gestured to the shelter from which he'd come. A tall girl with dark hair made her way over to her father's side. Lucas couldn't help but notice her limp. She glanced at his face for a moment, her blue eyes meeting his, before dropping shyly to the grass. Ingrid held out her right hand, keeping her left with its curled fingers, tucked against her waist.

Lucas took her hand, shaking it firmly but gently.

"His father is ill, Ingrid. I'd like you to go with him tomorrow and see what can be done for Joshua."

Lucas gulped. If he was to leave already tomorrow, and he should if Ingrid could truly be of help, he'd have to trade fast and furiously in the morning.

Her face broke out into a wide grin. She glanced at her father. "I get to meet Joshua? Then she turned her beaming smile on Lucas. "He's your father?"

Lucas nodded.

"He brought my mother out of the vault." She held her hands up, spreading her arms wide. "I've lived under the sky since my first breath because of him. What's it like, living with him?"

Sutton gave his daughter a quick hug. "I have to finish unpacking. Stay close by, will you?"

She nodded, pulling away from his arms and taking hold of one of Lucas's instead, leading him away as she started walking. Once they were walking together, he didn't notice her limp, or maybe he just adjusted for it without thinking. Many of the tenants in town had similar gaits, including his youngest sister.

"You've not come to trade before?" he asked, interrupting her flow of excited questions about the town and his father.

"I'm usually helping mother or one of the others with birthing. Just happened no one was near their time, and I've been begging to go for years. I think father said yes just to shut me up." She giggled. "You've been here before?"

"Every year since I could walk. My father claims I rode on his shoulders the first year. I think he was trying to get me to shut up, too."

Ingrid laughed. Her arm around his, her warm hand resting on his skin. They passed other shelters on their walk. The occupants waved to Lucas as they passed. Many stopped them to ask after Joshua and all sent wishes for his recovery.

He couldn't help but notice the thick raised brow of Jack Orrington as they passed by. He did ask after Joshua like the others, but when they spotted Orrington over at Sutton's shelter, it was clear he wasn't happy.

His raised voice carried in the open field. "Of all the underhanded schemes. You know full well, I was going to propose a match with my Jenny."

"He's not here, is he?" Sutton remained calm, sitting on his stool, sipping something steaming in a cup. A young boy sat by his side. He was far more affected by Orrington's tirade that his father. The boy blanched, his hand shaking, causing his cup to jiggle.

"So you toss Ingrid at his son before I even have a chance to talk to the boy?" His fists were clenched at his side and his neck flushed red.

"I did no such thing. Joshua is ill. I merely offered the services of my daughter."

Ingrid had gone quiet by his side, a state he'd come to suspect was unusual for her. Her grip on his arm tightened. She whispered, "You have to say something. Orrington has a terrible temper."

From what his father had said, all the Jacks did, but the cause for her concern was plain. Lucas untangled himself from Ingrid, wished fervently that his father was beside him, and then entered the arena.

Lucas forced himself to look Orrington in the eye. "Is Jenny here?"

Orrington halted whatever he was going to throw at Sutton next. "Yes, yes, she is."

"Might I meet her? I haven't made any decisions on a match, but I intend to before I leave."

Sutton looked concerned. He may have offered Ingrid with the intention of helping his father, but Lucas could clearly see that a match had also been on his mind.

Ingrid took the lapse in the conversation as an invitation to rejoin her father. He didn't look particularly pleased with her. She cast Lucas a pleading glance.

"Yes, of course," said Orrington. "She's helping unload the cart." Appeased, the red faded from his neck as he led Lucas away from Sutton and Ingrid.

"Jenny is a handy girl. You'll find her very useful."

Lucas remained silent, not wanting to commit himself to anything inadvertently. The swaths of matted down grass around the carts and shelters the fortress dwellers had commandeered indicated they'd been there since morning, or maybe even the night before.

He knew Jenny before Orrington said a word. A young girl, probably the same age as Teresa stood beside the cart, hefting bags of corn with ease. Her broad shoulders and square face matched her father's.

"I'll give you two some time to get acquainted,"

said Orrington, taking a bag under each arm and heading back to the shelter.

"Hello, Jenny," he said offering to take the next bag from her.

"Lucas." She nodded, tossing the bag to him.

He staggered under the weight, not expecting it from the way she easily lifted the bags. His father would have skipped the small talk and asked the obvious question. So that's what he did. "Your father has proposed a match between us. What are your thoughts?"

"I can help build things, hammer, lift, carry, you know?"

He nodded. "But what are you looking for in a match?"

She gave him a blank look. "A place to live?"

"You have that."

Jenny jumped down from the cart and took a quick look around for her father. Lucas joined her, spotting Orrington watching them with a determined gleam in his blue eyes from where he stood, arms crossed over his chest, just outside his shelter.

"Help me with the goat, will you?" Jenny asked.

"You have an extra goat?"

"No, but we can spare one if we have too. If you have something we really need, you know?" she said quietly.

Excited by the prospect of learning what trade goods he might ask more for, he took the rope for the goat. "What kind of things do you really need?"

"Fewer mouths. The soil is tired."

Cursed, from what Lucas knew of the horrors that had happened there, but he kept his opinions to himself. "How many brothers and sisters do you have?"

"Living? Two. An older brother and a younger."

"Your older brother, has he found a match yet?"

Jenny shook her head.

"How much older?"

"Fifteen. Year older than me."

"If you go back home, will your father be angry with you?"

She shook her head again. "He expected Joshua. He wanted to make a match. He was pretty sure he could convince him to take the deal. But you're not him. He has no history with you. Can't hold anything over your head, you know?"

"Your brother, he's like you?"

"Whole and strong, you mean?"

And blunt, apparently. "Yes, I suppose that's what I mean."

She nodded, hair brushing her shoulders as she did so.

"Then I have a deal for your father. I'm sorry, but I need Ingrid. My father is sick, and she might be able to help him."

Jenny let out a long sigh what sounded more like relief than despair. "And she's pretty. Even if she's not entirely whole."

"That wasn't the deciding factor," he said

quickly. Given a couple more years to grow into her body, Jenny might be quite a sight. And he certainly didn't want to be on her bad side, regardless. He'd need the favor of all the fortress dwellers in the future if he was to continue helping his father.

Jenny nudged him with her hip. "It's okay, really. I like home. Not that I mind you," she added with a downcast smile.

"Same here." He nudged her back. "Shall we break the news to your father?"

"I suppose we should. He's probably got all sorts of plans already lined up in his head. Better he doesn't get too far with them. That will just make him angrier."

Lucas nodded, striding back to Orrington with Jenny right behind. At least he had a few inches of stride on her.

"Well?" asked Orrington, looking more at Jenny than Lucas.

"I am prepared to propose a match, but not for Jenny."

"You're not getting the goat if you don't want my daughter."

His disgruntled leap of conversation took Lucas by surprise. "As much as I'd like your goat, that's not what I mean. I would like to propose that your eldest son visit my father. My sister is interested in making a match. If your son is anything like Jenny, I'm sure she'll like him. However, I'd rather she meet him herself before anything is agreed upon.

Orrington rubbed his stubbled chin. "I

wouldn't be opposed to that. I can have George to town in two weeks. Will that suit you?"

Lucas nodded. "And by then my father might be ready to take visitors again, and you can deal with him yourself."

Orrington's face brightened considerably. "You've got yourself a deal, Lucas."

Lucas said his farewells to Jenny and her father and then returned to the camp his people had set up during his absence. Most were already finishing their evening meal. He was impressed to see that his efficient crew had unloaded the wagon and all the trade goods had been lined up to remove from their packaging at first light. He hadn't even had to supervise. His father had trained them all well.

As the sun sunk nearer the horizon, those that had finished eating slipped through camp, visiting others, and surveying the possible matches as he'd done.

With some time alone, Lucas located an unoccupied shelter and sorted through his sack to find something to eat. He'd just finished the chicken pie that Teresa had packed for him when he heard hesitant footsteps approaching.

The wooden structure was completely open on one long side and enclosed on the other three. The roof overhead, though aged, was still in good shape and watertight. Not that he'd hoped to have an occasion to test that. The sky looked clear above Ingrid's head. She'd braided her hair, and was now playing with the end of the braid, wrapping the blonde hair around her finger.

"Sutton send you?" he asked after taking a deep drink from his canteen.

"No. I couldn't sleep until I knew. Have you decided?"

"I have to talk to your father first, but yes."

"Orrington was looking quite pleased. My father is concerned."

"So he *did* send you."

She shook her head. "No, but I need to know."

Lucas decided that he shouldn't torture her, even if he hadn't talked to her father first. "He has no reason to be concerned."

"Really?" She dropped her braid, clasping her hands together.

"Yes, really. Do you really think you can help my father?"

"From what you've told me, I've helped a woman with the same symptoms. I'll need to find a few things, but I'm guessing you have them, carrots, garlic, and ginger?"

Feeling a weight lift off his shoulders, Lucas nodded.

"There are a few other things we can try too if those don't help him enough, but we can start there."

"Thank you. You should get back before it gets too dark to see."

"I'll see you in the morning then." She leaned over to give him a peck on the cheek before leaving.

The sounds of the others settling in around him for the night filled the air. The chill of nightfall fell upon him as the last remnants of the day faded from the sky. Lucas shook out the blanket from his sack and wrapped it around himself as he settled down against the rear wall of the shelter. It was then he missed his father most. His warmth, his shoulder that was both pillow and assurance that all was well with the world. The steady breathing that lulled him to sleep. Tonight, for the first time, he was truly alone. But tomorrow, he wouldn't be ever again. Lucas drifted off to sleep with the chirping of the night bugs and the memory of Ingrid's kiss.

Morning brought a flurry of activity, readying the wares for trade and surveying what the scavengers and fortress dwellers had brought. After his initial round of the trade tables, Lucas sent off some of his people with offers. Meanwhile, he supervised the transactions at the town table, nodding or shaking his head when his people came to him for approval on questionable offers. Once the main flurry of trading was complete, the more serious business of matches began.

He'd already dealt with Orrington and would address Sutton shortly, but it was adding his approval to the proposed matches of the townspeople that required his attention first. His father had instructed him to build the town, not let his people be convinced to leave any more than necessary, but sometimes it was necessary to keep populations in balance. Since they'd left the confines of the fortress and mingled with the scavengers, the bloodlines had slowly begun to improve. His father suspected the food they grew far from the cursed ground of the fortress also had something to do with the improvement.

Two scavenger families, after concluding their trades, had requested to become tenants. Three other families had asked to take up temporary residence at the trade land through winter, fortifying several of the simple shelters as payment. Someday, Lucas thought, the trade land might become another town, one more place where those who straggled in from the wildlands to settle down and learn to become civilized again. More came every year as stories of Joshua's town were shared around fires.

"So," said Sutton, approaching him at last.

Lucas stood tall before the giant man. "I would like to take Ingrid for my wife if you would find our match agreeable."

Sutton grinned. "I would. And in trade?"

Lucas surveyed the goods that were left on the wagon and ran through those in his bag that he'd packed for this occasion. But nothing struck him as quite right. "I would invite you and your family to join us as tenants. We will build you a house of your own."

"I have a house of my own," stated Sutton, looking from Lucas to Ingrid.

"You also have a family to feed, and if you have more children, your wife will want Ingrid around."

Sutton's lips curled into the slightest smile. "You are your father's son."

"We could use your strong back," Lucas said

gamily. "I had to let Jenny go, her strength would have been an asset to the town."

Sutton actually laughed. Lucas couldn't remember hearing a Jack laugh before. "She would have. That's one solid girl. I suppose I'll have to do. When will you have a place ready for us?"

Lucas surveyed those that had pledged to become tenants. In addition to the two scavenger families, there were three couples, one with a baby, from the fortress. Most of them had an impairment of some sort, but seemed, on the whole, healthy and eager.

"We have enough temporary housing to get all of you through winter. Your own home might have to wait until spring. But you'll eat well until then."

He sighed inwardly, realizing his own home would have to wait longer, but there was room in his father's house for one more.

"I heard a rumor Orrington was to visit your father in two week's time."

"It's true."

"It will take some time to conclude my business in the fortress. Perhaps we will travel with him."

"I'm glad you're coming too." Ingrid hugged her father and then returned to Lucas's side.

With business concluded, Lucas signaled for the horses to be hitched up to the wagons and all the goods they'd traded for to be loaded. He also found room for the mother and her baby to ride among the sacks of corn.

Lucas took the rope for the horses. Ingrid

walked at his side. As they departed, he looked over his shoulder at the next wave of immigrants. The satisfied feeling of a job well done along with the giddiness of his new future bounced around in his stomach. He wondered if his father had felt the same way, traveling this same road sixteen years before. Knowing his father and mother, they had both been too busy smiling at one another to pay much attention to the uncertainty that had lain before them. A far more secure future would soon be his.

OTHER BOOKS BY JEAN DAVIS

A collection of short speculative fiction featuring stories published from 2010 to 2017.

Sahmara, an escaped slave in an enemy country, prays for help, but the assistance of the gods has a price. Along with her lovers Olando and Sara, she may be the one to help take her homeland back if she can only find the strength within herself.

Abducting the angry and suicidal god of war might not be Logan's wisest choice, but she's the weapon that might be able to defeat the army of Matouk, who destroyed his homeworld. If he can show her how to love, they might save each other from the terrors that plague his nights and all of her days.

Available in print and ebook
Like a book? Please consider leaving a review.

ABOUT THE AUTHOR

Jean Davis lives in West Michigan with her musical husband, two nerdy teenagers, and two attention-craving terriers. When not ruining fictional lives from the comfort of her writing chair, she can be found devouring books and sushi, enjoying the offerings of local breweries, weeding her flower garden, or picking up hundreds of sticks while attempting to avoid the abundant snake population that also shares her yard. She writes an array of speculative fiction. Her novels include *A Broken Race*, *Sahmara*, *The Last God*. Follow her writing adventures and sign up for her newsletter at www.jeanddavis.blogspot.com.

87154507R00145

Made in the USA
Lexington, KY
20 April 2018